PASTOR'S PRIZE

CULPEPPER COWBOYS BOOK 15

KIRSTEN OSBOURNE

UNLIMITED DREAMS

Copyright © 2017 by Kirsten Osbourne

Unlimited Dreams Publishing

All rights reserved.

Cover design by Erin Dameron Hill/ EDH Graphics

No part of this book may be reproduced in any form or by any electronic or mechanical means including information storage and retrieval systems, without permission in writing from the author. The only exception is by a reviewer, who may quote short excerpts in a review.

This book is a work of fiction. Names, characters, places, and incidents either are products of the author's imagination or are used fictitiously. Any resemblance to actual persons, living or dead, events, or locales is entirely coincidental.

Kirsten Osbourne

Visit my website at www.kirstenandmorganna.com

Printed in the United States of America

INTRODUCTION

Rikki Dobson has spent her whole life living in her famous sister's shadow. When she moves to Culpepper, Wyoming to recover from a harrowing experience, it's the last place in the world she expects to find love. Working at a bakery with three loving women makes life easier, but she's still afraid of the world around her. When Pastor Benjamin, the handsome new associate pastor sits beside her in church, she doesn't know whether to be happy or frightened.

Ben Norton isn't looking for love. He's happy with his new job as assistant pastor and counselor for a small church in Culpepper. He's met the beautiful Rikki a couple of times, but it isn't until he sits beside her one morning that he realizes there is something more to her than meets the eye. Will Rikki be able to overcome her fears? Or will the two of them spend the rest of their lives alone?

1

Rikki Dobson pulled into the small church's parking lot, snagging one of the last parking spaces at the very back. She would be late if she didn't rush, but that was how she liked it. She didn't want to have to stand around before or after church making small talk. Being around men frightened her. She'd had a very tough year, and she didn't want to have to mingle and act like she was enjoying herself when she just wanted to get away as soon as the service was over.

She found a seat in the back row and sat down just as the music started. She'd timed it perfectly. She stood and watched the words on the giant screen, singing along. She loved to sing, and she was very good at it, but she never did it in front of anyone.

"Would you mind scooting over one chair?" a deep voice asked from behind her.

Rikki felt a shiver run through her. It didn't matter whose voice it was. A man was standing altogether too close to her. She turned and saw that it was Pastor Benjamin, the new assistant pastor. Well, not terribly new. He'd been in town since August, but that still seemed new. She'd been in town a few months longer than he had, and she was still a newcomer herself.

Rikki moved over three chairs, giving him plenty of room, so she wouldn't have to sit too close to him or anyone else. Having people in her space made her very uncomfortable.

He gave her a questioning look as he set his things down and turned to the front of the church, his eyes going to the screen. He sang, his baritone voice sounding more like a rumble than a voice raised in song.

Rikki kept her eyes on Brother Anthony through the whole service, carefully avoiding looking at Pastor Benjamin. Brother Anthony was an older man who didn't seem to be able to do anything with decorum while Pastor Benjamin was...well...how did one describe Pastor Benjamin? He was sexy and took Rikki's breath away. *Was it wrong to think of a pastor as sexy?*

Brother Anthony's sermon was about tolerance, and Rikki thoroughly enjoyed listening to the man talk on the subject. As soon as the service was over, she quickly gathered her things to make a rapid escape.

She'd just shrugged into her coat when Pastor Benjamin asked, "Are you going out with a group for lunch?"

Rikki shook her head, putting her scarf around her shoulders. "No, I'll probably just go home for lunch." She was truly surprised to hear her voice say the words. She was seldom able to get out an entire sentence in a social situation. At least she was getting better at being able to talk to people at the bakery while she was working.

"You should come to Bob's with me then. There's no reason for you to sit home alone."

She frowned. "Thanks for the offer, but I don't really do well in crowded places."

Ben studied the pretty girl in front of him, wondering why she looked so skittish. He'd heard rumors that something bad had happened to her but he had no idea what it was. "You won't get comfortable in crowds unless you're in them some. Isolating yourself will just make things worse." He didn't speak from experience, but he'd taken enough psychology classes on his way to his masters of psychology that he knew what he was talking about. Being a minister wasn't just a calling for him. It was his passion...his everything.

"Thank you, Pastor, but I know my limits. I've been here too long already."

Ben watched as she hurried out of the church. He knew little about Rikki, other than her name and that she never socialized with people after church. Suddenly he wanted to know more—no, he *needed* to know more.

He saw Grace Wells, formerly Grace Quinlan watching him, and he nodded to her, slowly making his way through the crowd to her side. "What do you know about Rikki Dobson that I don't?"

Grace shrugged. "Everyone knows her story."

"Everyone? Meaning the whole town is gossiping about it?"

"Everyone meaning she's been talked about on the news and her story has been in all the papers—and not just the gossip rags." Grace shook her head. "You really don't know what happened to her?"

Ben frowned. "I don't know anything about it. Tell me what happened."

Grace sighed. "Do you know who Valerie Savoy is?"

"Of course. Everyone knows who Valerie Savoy is."

Valerie was the star of a night time drama filmed in Texas. The show was called *Lazy Love*, and while he wasn't an avid watcher, he'd caught a few episodes.

"You know Rikki is her kid sister, right?"

Ben's eyes widened. "I wondered why she looked so familiar!" Rikki looked a great deal like her older sister. He thought for a moment and then sighed. "Wait, didn't Valerie's kid sister get kidnapped earlier this year?"

Grace nodded. "Yes, she did."

"That explains a lot. I assume Rikki is the sister who got kidnapped."

"Yeah, she is. She's had a really hard time since. In fact, she moved to Culpepper so she could get away from people in her town always talking about her. She works at the bakery with my cousins and me."

"I've seen her sister here a few times, but she's not a regular church-goer."

Grace smiled. "She's regular when she's in town. They film three weeks on and one week off. She's always here on her weeks off."

"Oh." Ben frowned. "I need to learn more about the people here. I got to Culpepper and jumped into counseling with both feet, but I haven't really taken the time to get to know the people who don't need counseling. I should do that soon."

"Rikki needs it, but I doubt she'll go. She told me that she did a little bit of counseling before she left Iowa for Culpepper, but she didn't feel like it helped her so she stopped it when she moved here. She seems to be getting better in very small increments. She doesn't jump every time we laugh any longer."

"Sounds like she's having a rough time of it." He rubbed the back of his neck. "I should reach out to her." As the associate pastor and designated counselor of the church, it fell to him to worry about the mental health of the congregants.

"I saw the two of you talking a little while ago. That's the most I've ever seen her talk to a man outside the bakery."

"What do you mean? She can't totally avoid talking to men."

Grace shrugged. "And yet she seems to. I'm sure she's talked to Roy Williams a bit, but he's probably the only one. She sneaks into church at the last second and leaves as soon as it's over. She's afraid of men."

"And you say she works at the bakery?" Ben asked, knowing he needed to at least reach out to the girl.

"Yup. She comes in at ten and stays 'til we close at six. She's been a good employee, and she's learning to ice the cakes beautifully."

"I'll come by tomorrow then."

Grace nodded, her face full of skepticism. "I'm not sure she'll like that, but it's probably a good idea. She needs someone to talk to her about her fears."

Marcus Wells, Brother Anthony's grandson, walked over then, his eyes full of love as he looked at his beautiful wife. "Are you ready to go?"

"Yup. Are we heading to Bob's Burger Barn?"

"Of course. I can't remember where we ate on Sundays before he opened that place."

"At the diner, of course." Grace nodded to Ben. "It was good talking to you Pastor Benjamin."

"Call me Ben." He'd had enough of being called Pastor Benjamin by everyone in town.

"All right, Ben. Have a good day, and I hope to see you at the bakery soon." She slipped her hand into Marcus's and the two of them headed for the door at the back of the church.

Ben watched them go, a look of longing on his face. He wanted what Marcus and Grace had. He'd wanted it for a long time, but things hadn't worked out for him.

———

Rikki drove to the Culpepper ranch on autopilot. Why had Pastor Benjamin been talking to her? Had someone told him that she needed counseling? She did, and she even knew she did, but she didn't want it. Shouldn't it be her choice whether or not she had her head shrunk?

When she got to the ranch, she parked beside Linda Culpepper's blue SUV. Getting out of her small car, she hurried to the door as if someone was chasing her. She hated being outside around her car. It made her feel so exposed! She knew it was crazy, because there was no one lurking in the bushes on the Culpepper ranch to kidnap her and throw her into the trunk of a car, but she couldn't get the fear out of her mind. What Curtis had done to her would forever be in her mind.

She accidentally slammed the door against the wall in her rush to get inside, and Linda came out of the kitchen, smiling. "I'm glad you're home. Lunch?"

Rikki struggled to slow her breathing down. This was the hardest part of going on after the kidnapping—remembering that there *wasn't* someone out there waiting to hurt her. "Lunch sounds nice," she finally said, when she could. Linda would understand though. She'd been her confidante and friend since Rikki had moved in with her a few months before. She still lived at her sister's ranch in her little garage apartment the week out of the month Valerie wasn't filming, but the rest of the time, she was there with Linda. She felt safer with another woman around.

"I made soup." Linda walked to the kitchen and dished up two bowls of soup, carrying them to the table. "Would you get out the silverware?"

Rikki walked into the kitchen and pulled the utensils from the drawers. She helped out around the house some, but Linda had always refused to let her pay any rent or help with groceries. It made Rikki feel guilty, because she made a decent wage at the bakery and had no other expenses.

"Pastor Benjamin invited me to go out after church today," Rikki said, surprising herself. She rarely volunteered information about her day, usually waiting for the older woman to ask questions before divulging information.

"He did? You didn't want to go?" Linda gave her a knowing look that made Rikki wish she could show the whole world how wrong they were about her. If they *were* wrong, she would do it in a heartbeat.

Rikki sighed. "You know I think I wanted to go a little bit. It's the first time I've even been tempted."

Linda smiled at her. "I think that's a really good positive step. Maybe you should have said yes."

"Maybe. Not this time, though."

"Pastor Benjamin is a handsome man."

Rikki blushed a little, shrugging. She'd thought the same thing just a short while before. "Is he? I didn't notice," she fibbed. She was noticing a man for the first time since the kidnapping, and she wasn't sure she liked it. It was odd to notice a man when she was afraid of them. How could she be thinking in terms of how nice he was to look at when she was supposed to be hiding under a rock?

"You did notice!" Linda said, her whole face lighting up. "You need to go out with him if he asks again."

"He was just asking me to go out with a group."

"Did he say that?"

Rikki shook her head. "Well, no, but what else would he want with me? I'm messed up in the head and everyone knows it. I'm nobody's prize."

"You need to see yourself the way the rest of the world sees you, Rikki. Wasn't Valerie voted one of Hollywood Magazine's most beautiful women of the year? You look a lot like your sister!"

"Yeah, on the outside we do look the same. People can see the darkness inside me though." Rikki sat at the table and picked up her spoon, taking a bite of the soup. "This is delicious."

Linda obviously knew it was pointless to continue the conversation, because she sat down and ate as well. "I'm going out with Roy tonight. Are you going to be all right home alone?"

"As long as I know you'll be back, I'll be fine." Rikki knew she'd be locking all the doors as soon as Linda left, and she'd be frightened the whole time, but she had to learn to be alone sometime. She was simply grateful for the opportunity to live with someone while she learned how. She could easily have stayed with her mother in Iowa, but the whole town suddenly felt different—dangerous. She hadn't been able to go back to work at the grocery store— the scene of her kidnapping—since the incident.

"Feel free to fix yourself anything you want," Linda said unnecessarily. Rikki knew she had the freedom to do anything she wanted in the house.

"Thanks." Rikki concentrated on her meal after that, not wanting to think about the evening ahead. She hated being alone—almost as much as she hated being in a crowd.

BEN MADE a point to stop by the bakery for lunch the following day. He knew they did a brisk business in the mornings, but he'd heard that they were rarely busy at lunch time, because Bob's Burger Barn tended to draw a large lunch crowd.

He walked into the bakery for the first time, looking around him. He was amazed at the small business. Four women worked there, all of them visible from the front of the building.

Stepping up to the display, he smiled at Rikki, who was manning the counter. "I've heard really good things about the kolaches here. Would you recommend the sausage or ham? Or the plain cheese?"

"I like the ham," Rikki responded, feeling a lot more comfortable with a counter between them.

"Give me three of the ham then."

"Do you want them warmed?" she asked, removing three of the savory pastries and setting them on a paper plate.

"Yes, please." Ben leaned against the counter as he watched her efficient motions. She had obviously performed the service hundreds of times. "I'd like coffee to go with that as well."

"Of course." She walked to the coffee pot and picked up a mug, before looking at him. "Is this for here or to go? I guess I should have asked that." She blushed at her error. What was it about the man that turned her into a bumbling fool? It wasn't just that he was a man, because she didn't blush for most men. Only him.

When she set the food in front of him, and gave him his total, he pulled his wallet out. "Why don't you join me?"

Rikki's eyes widened in surprise. She shook her head,

refusing without thought. She couldn't sit with him while he ate.

From behind her, Grace called, "It's time for you to take a break, Rikki. Join him!"

Rikki turned and glared at Grace, but followed her instructions. She poured herself a cup of hot chocolate and grabbed a muffin before following him. They went into the dining room, and she sat at one of the small tables, doing her best not to meet his eyes. She hoped he didn't realize that Grace was trying to play matchmaker, because it seemed very obvious.

Ben looked around the small, immaculate dining room. "You're not busy," he said, stating the obvious. He needed to make her comfortable if he was going to get her to open up to him. She wasn't his client, so he wasn't sure why it was so important to him, but it was.

"Not at this time of day. We used to have a small lunch crowd, but since Bob opened his place in town, it's pretty quiet here at this time of day." Rikki broke off a piece of her muffin top and popped it into her mouth. The orange flavor exploded on her tongue, and she thanked God that Patience had decided to experiment with some new recipes. This one was a winner. She made a mental note to tell the other girl after lunch.

Ben took a bite of his kolache, closing his eyes as he savored the taste. "This is fabulous. Do you help make these?"

She shook her head. "Nope. Those are all Patience. I've learned to help with the icing of the cakes and cookies, but I haven't been given the task of baking the kolaches yet."

"How do you like living in Culpepper?" he asked.

She shrugged. "It's nice. I wish my sister and brother-in-law were around more, but I enjoy living with Linda."

"You stay with Linda Culpepper while they're filming, right?"

Rikki nodded. "You learned a lot about me in a short period of time."

He frowned. "It's not hard. This is a gossipy little town. Not in a bad way, but everyone knows everyone else's business. And your story isn't exactly a secret."

She sighed. "No, it's not. My face was on the front page of a whole lot of newspapers when it first happened, and again when he settled without going to trial."

"Do you want to talk about what happened?"

She shrugged. "What is there to talk about? I was kidnapped. My sister saved me."

"There's more to it than that. Not a lot of details were released about what happened to you. Did he rape you?" He knew the words were blunt, but he also knew that there were times when you had to just say what was on your mind to get to the needed answers.

She shook her head. She didn't want to talk about it. It was still painful. "No, he didn't."

"How did you get away?"

She frowned at him. "You can find those details in at least thirty places online. Why don't you do a search?"

"I don't want to do a search. I want you to tell me."

"Look, Pastor Benjamin, I'm not sure why you've decided to make me your project, but I really don't want to talk about it. It's not easy, and if you hadn't noticed, I'm at my place of business."

"Call me Ben."

"Excuse me?"

"Call me Ben. I'm not talking to you as a pastor. I'm talking as a friend." And he was, which surprised him. He'd told himself he wanted to make sure she was all right, because that's what a pastor did, which was true as far as it went. No, he was interested in her in a much more base level than as a pastor talking to a congregant. He was just interested in her. Period.

"Why should I call you Ben? You're trying to counsel me. I can't call my counselor Ben."

"I'm not trying to counsel you, though." He reached over and covered her hand with his. "I want to get to know you better, but not as a pastor."

She blinked at him a few times, before slowly responding, her face flushed with embarrassment. "I'm not sure I understand. I thought Brother Anthony told you to talk to me."

He shook his head. "Not at all. Brother Anthony only knows I left for lunch. He has no idea where I am, or that I'm trying to talk to you."

"But—I don't understand why you're here then. Why me?"

"I can't be the first man to tell you that you're a beautiful woman, Rikki."

"Well, no, but you know what happened to me!"

"Is that supposed to scare me away? The fact that you were kidnapped?"

She shrugged. "It scares everyone else away. No one knows what to say to me. It's like I've become someone else after what happened." And she hated it. She hated that people looked at her and saw a victim. People once saw her as Valerie Dobson's little sister, and she'd thought that was rough. Now that she was the younger sister who was kidnapped, she knew that she'd had it easy before.

"It's not scaring me. I think you're a special woman, and I want to spend more time with you. Would you be willing to go out with me?"

Rikki stared at him for a minute, her voice lost. She'd never really dated. She'd never had the time. She'd been an honor's student in high school, studying all the time. Then she'd gone to college for pre-med, so she was again studying all the time. She'd decided a year off was necessary after the kidnapping though, so there she was in Culpepper, trying to remember what she used to see that was so good in the world.

"Well?" he asked, wondering why it mattered to him so much that this girl went out with him. Sure, she was beautiful, but he'd met other beautiful women that he hadn't felt compelled to date. She was different, though.

"I guess I can do that." She couldn't believe she'd agreed. As soon as the words were out of her mouth, she wished them back. She couldn't go out with a pastor. Why would he want *her*?

Ben smiled. "Tonight?"

"Tonight...I...Sure. I guess tonight is fine."

"I'll pick you up at seven." He stood, crumpling the trash from his lunch and carrying it to the garbage can.

"What should I wear?" she asked, stunned at how quickly he was pushing forward.

"Jeans are fine. See you then." He waved as he left the building, leaving Rikki staring after him.

She wasn't sure why she'd agreed, but there was no going back now. She would have to go out with the handsome new pastor, but she was sure he would go away soon. She was nobody's prize, and he'd realize it faster than she could recount the story of what had happened to her.

2

Rikki began to panic before she even got home from work that afternoon. She knew there was no way she could be alone with a man. What had she been thinking?

As soon as she walked in the door, she headed straight for Linda, confessing what she'd agreed to. "When Ben comes to the door, will you tell him I'm dead? Please?"

Linda frowned at Rikki. "He'll realize you're not dead when you show up for church on Sunday."

"I'll change churches! How far of a drive is it to Haskell?" Rikki asked, naming the nearest town.

"You're not going to change churches. Let's take this one step at a time. Go to your room and change into jeans and a nice shirt."

Rikki bit her lip, nodding slowly. "I can do that much."

"Then go." Linda reached out and gave Rikki a slight push in the direction of her bedroom. "When you're done, come out and we'll talk."

Rikki hurried to her room, digging through her clothes. Jeans. She knew she had a pair of jeans somewhere. Several in fact. She found a pair hanging in her closet, and took them out, and then she found a nice green blouse that matched her eyes. She changed and then went back out to find Linda in the living room. "I did it." Why did she feel like changing her clothes was such an accomplishment?

Linda smiled, assessing the younger woman's appearance. "You have a bit of flour on your cheek. Go wash your face and put some lipstick on. Thankfully, you don't need any more makeup than that."

Rikki hurried off to do as she was told. She noticed that her hair was still in the ponytail she'd put it in for work, so she brushed it out, letting it fall in waves down her back. Her hair was much longer than she'd ever worn it, but she couldn't force herself to sit with anyone standing over her with scissors. It hadn't been cut since the kidnapping.

She hurried back out into the living room, certain she was ready to go now. All except her coat, and that was on the back of the couch. She sat down beside Linda. "I'm scared. What if I freak out about being alone with him?"

"Does he know your history?"

"He knows about the kidnapping. I'm sure by now he's searched every news site that covered what happened." Rikki didn't have to talk about how much she hated that the incident was online, just waiting for everyone to read. Linda understood.

"If he knows what happened to you, then he should be able to handle it if you do get scared. He's a counselor, and from what I hear, he's a very good one."

Rikki sighed. "You know I never just 'get scared.' I have a full-on panic attack!"

"If it happens, he'll deal with it. That's what he does, after all."

"I just wish I didn't have to worry about those things! I'm

still afraid to get in and out of my car!" Rikki shook her head.

"I know you are. But I also know you *want* to get better. Hiding here at my house and avoiding all possibilities of a relationship isn't going to help you in any way."

"Why do you always have to be so logical?" Rikki jumped at the doorbell. "That's probably him! I can't go! I just—There's no way I can handle it. Not tonight."

Linda squeezed Rikki's hand. "Then tell him that, but I'm not going to do it for you. Go to the door and let him know you can't go."

Rikki wrinkled her nose, knowing Linda was right. She hurried to the door and threw it open, wanting to get it over with. She stood staring in shock when she saw who was there. Grace stood with Marcus and Ben. Rikki blinked a few times. "Do you want to come in?"

Grace laughed softly. "We're here to get you for your date tonight. Ben got take-out and we're eating at our house."

Rikki nodded, hurrying to get her coat. He'd handled her fears. She wondered if he'd always know what to do to keep her from getting scared. "I won't be too late," she told Linda.

Linda smiled in response. "Just have a good time."

She shrugged into her coat and walked out to the car with Ben at her side. "Where'd the others go?"

"They're waiting in the car. I thought it would seem strange if all three of us were standing there waiting for you to come out."

"It was strange that all three of you came to pick me up to begin with."

He opened the back door of Grace's vehicle for her, before walking around to the other side. "I thought you might be getting nervous, and you'd feel better if Grace was there as well. She's agreed to come with me to drop you off if you need her to."

Rikki bit her lip. "Can I get back to you on that?" She wanted to say she'd be fine, but the truth was she didn't know how she'd be in a couple of hours. At least she knew Grace and her husband Marcus, so she wouldn't be nervous about being in their home.

Ben nodded solemnly. "Of course, you can. I'm just glad you agreed to come out with me to begin with."

Marcus looked into the rearview mirror. "Everyone buckled?"

Rikki quickly buckled her seatbelt. She didn't like wearing them, because she felt like they pinned her down, making it harder to get away. "I am now."

On the short drive to Marcus and Grace's house, Grace talked about the baby shower cake she was making for her sisters Joy and Faith, who were having a joint shower. They were due on the same day, which Rikki found to be very odd. "I'll bet Linda is bouncing off the walls getting ready for her first two grandbabies."

Rikki smiled at that. "She is. I think she's crocheted more little booties than anyone has ever crocheted. And she's painted little signs for their walls. I wish the girls would tell what they're having."

"I know! I think they just like knowing something no one else does." Grace shook her head. "My sisters can be pains at times." Both of the sisters in question were married to Culpepper sons. The Quinlan quadruplets had all married Culpeppers, and their younger sisters, twins Grace and Honor, had come out later and married men from Culpepper along with their two cousins. All eight of the former Quinlan girls now lived in Culpepper.

"All sisters can be pains at times!" Rikki said, only half joking.

"Even Valerie?" Grace asked, her eyes wide as she turned in her seat to look at Rikki.

"Especially Valerie! How would you like to be the younger sister of someone as famous as Valerie? Everyone knows her name. That's why I started going by Rikki. Both of us having V names was a pain, because then people really lumped us together."

"A V name?" Ben asked, a frown on his face. "Veronica?"

Rikki nodded. "I changed my name when I started high school, though, and refused to answer to Veronica anymore. Valerie was halfway through college then and everyone was convinced she was perfect."

"She's not?" Grace asked.

Rikki sighed. "I know you're a huge fan of Valerie's, but she really can be a pain. I hate living in her shadow."

Ben shrugged. "I'll have you know I have only seen the show a couple of times, and I'm not that fond of it."

Rikki frowned at him. "My sister is an incredible actress!"

He sighed. "I can't win either way, can I?"

"Probably not." She shook her head, laughing at herself. Only she was allowed to admit her sister was less than her impeccable reputation. "I love my sister, and no one gets to talk badly about her except me!"

"I still can't figure out why she's not perfect," Grace put in from the front seat. "I think she's pretty incredible."

"She is," Rikki agreed. "She'd do anything for me. I just wish I really was more like her at times."

"Why?" Ben asked. "You seem pretty awesome to me just the way you are."

"You don't understand. Valerie isn't just an actress. She

was a straight A student. Always the smartest girl in school. Always good at everything she touches. I felt so boring trying to live up to her perfection."

"I have an older brother. I understand completely."

"What does he do?" Rikki asked. Ben seemed rather perfect to her, so she couldn't imagine him trying to live up to someone else.

"He's a cardiac surgeon. Mom wanted us both to be doctors, but my calling was different." He shrugged. Sometimes he felt guilty for following his heart, and not becoming a doctor like his father and brother.

"I was pre-med before the kidnapping," she said softly, surprising herself. She rarely talked about what her plans were before, because she'd abandoned everything. It was all she could do to just survive at this point.

"Do you have plans to return to school?"

She shook her head. "Not at this time. I can't be around crowds. Or closed in places. Or cars."

"Cars?" He understood the first two, but cars?

"I was walking out to my car after a late shift at the grocery store where I worked when he grabbed me. Actually, he didn't have to grab me. He talked me into going with him. I was so gullible." She never would be again, though. She looked at everyone, wondering what they would do to her if given the chance. She missed the trust she used to be able to place in people.

"So now you're afraid of cars?"

"Well, that's inaccurate. I'm afraid of getting in and out of cars by myself. If I get out of my car and park it, even in broad daylight, I run to wherever I'm going. It's silly, but I expect him to jump out from behind every bush."

He frowned. He'd researched her to find out everything he could about what had happened. He'd thought he was going to try to get her into a counseling session, but he found he couldn't. His feelings for her were too strong to try to work with her. It wouldn't be professional. "Isn't he in jail?"

"He'll be in jail for a very long time. That doesn't change my fears. I know they're irrational."

He reached over and took her tiny hand in his. He was a large man. Over six two, and she was small. She couldn't have been much over five feet. She must feel dwarfed by him. He threaded his fingers through hers. "Okay?" he asked softly.

Rikki looked down at her hand in his and nodded. She was surprised by how very okay it felt to have her hand in his. "Yeah. It's good."

Marcus shut off the engine. "Food. And I thought we could play a card game. Anyone play euchre? Or is that just me?"

Rikki grinned. "I love euchre!"

Ben nodded. "I'm from a small town in Wisconsin. Euchre was what you did on Saturday nights if you weren't a drinker."

"I'm not sure how that follows, but okay!" Rikki said with a grin. "You play, Grace?"

"Marcus taught me. Should we play girls against the guys? I think we could take them, don't you?"

Rikki nodded with a grin. "I love that idea!"

Ben shook his head at her. "As long as you don't mind losing, her team is the perfect place to be!"

"Are pastors allowed to talk smack?" Rikki asked. "Isn't that against the law or something?"

"Oh, you hush. Pastors can do whatever they want as long as they're not being immoral."

Rikki was surprised at how comfortable she felt

throughout the meal. Ben sat beside her, and they shared a large order of fries from Bob's Burger Barn. "I hope you like burgers," he said.

"As long as you're not making me eat tacos, we're good."

Ben tilted his head to one side in confusion. "You don't like tacos? What do you eat on Tuesdays?"

"I usually love tacos, but my sister is very pregnant, and every time I see her, she's forcing tacos on me. I can't handle any more tacos!"

"I think I can understand that. Is she always eating tacos like that? Or is this a pregnancy thing?"

"It's a pregnancy thing, which is good, because if she was like this all the time, I might have to kick her."

Ben frowned. "Are you threatening violence against a pregnant woman?"

"Yes, I am. I really am."

"Wow." He was happy to see she could joke about her sister. She always seemed so serious that he was worried she never smiled.

"What made you decide to come to Culpepper?" she asked, surprised at her ability to speak with this man without tripping all over her tongue.

He shrugged. "I was finishing up at seminary, and I heard there was a need of a pastor with counseling experience here. I have a masters of psychology, and I knew that I would be able to be of help. So, I applied and got the job."

"Do you like working with Brother Anthony?" she asked. From what she'd seen the older man was very scattered when it came to sermons, weddings, and everything else he did.

"You should ask me that when his grandson isn't sitting across the table from me," Ben answered with a grin.

"Really, though, I enjoy the man. He makes me laugh, and keeps everyone on their toes."

"That's putting it mildly," Marcus said, shaking his head. "I wish I could say that it's old age, but he's always been that way. He says whatever pops into his head whenever he thinks it, and he sure can't remember anyone's name. He does well to remember mine!"

Rikki smiled. "I think that's my favorite thing about church here. I love it when he calls to your grandmother in the middle of a sermon. It feels so natural."

Ben laughed. "The first time I heard him do that, I thought he'd lost his mind, but the whole congregation acted like it was normal, so I went with it. Now I know it *is* normal around here."

"I thought all pastors did that," Marcus said. "Imagine my surprise when I went away to college and the pastor wasn't asking his wife questions constantly in the middle of his sermons. It felt like something was missing!"

Rikki grinned. "It would."

Grace shook her head. "I didn't know what to think! I come from a very religious family, and we've always attended churches that were very serious. There was absolutely no joking or asking questions of your wife during sermons at that church. I felt like I was in the Twilight Zone during my first few services, and I wasn't even supposed to know what that was!"

"You weren't allowed to watch the Twilight Zone?"

Grace rolled her eyes. "Don't get me started!"

Rikki eyed her employer. "Was it the same for Patience and Felicity?"

"In a way. Their mother didn't buy into all the religious nonsense, so it was a bit easier for them. They were homeschooled, and they got away with a lot during the day while their dad was at work. We went to a church-run school. There was nothing frivolous in our lives."

"I'm sorry. I can't imagine having a life without laughter."

Grace smiled. "We laughed. A lot. Just not when our parents were around. Trust me, we figured out how to do everything we wanted to do."

Rikki looked back at Ben. "So how long have you known you wanted to be a pastor?"

He shrugged. "I went to a religious college, not because I was religious, but because that's where I was given a scholarship. I dedicated my life to Christ there, and I knew I wanted to devote my life to Him almost immediately."

"And are you glad you did?"

"I am. I can't imagine where I'd be if I wasn't in Culpepper. It's a special place."

"I can't wait until they light up the town square. Linda says it's the most beautiful Christmas display I'll ever see!" Rikki loved Christmas. It had always been her favorite holiday, and she refused to let this year be any different, just because she'd been through a traumatic experience.

"Are you going to the tree lighting then?" He'd heard there was a festival around the tree lighting, and he was planning to be there. He'd love to have her at his side.

Rikki shook her head. "No, I really can't do crowds. I might watch from my car." With the doors locked, but she didn't need to add that. She knew the others understood without her saying it.

After they had eaten, Rikki helped with the few dishes they'd dirtied before they sat down to play euchre. Rikki had grown up playing the game, but she hadn't encountered many who knew it.

At the end of the night, Grace and Rikki had won two

games to the men's one. They fist bumped across the table and Grace made a face at Marcus. "Told you we'd win!"

Marcus rolled his eyes at her. "You just learned to play. How can you be so confident that you'd win?"

Rikki glanced at the clock, surprised by how late it was. "I need to go. My boss will not be happy with me if I'm not on time tomorrow!"

Grace laughed. "Since your boss probably won't be on time, maybe she won't notice!"

"If you don't notice, Patience or Felicity will!" Rikki got to her feet. "Thank you for having me over. I really had a good time."

Ben got to his feet as well. "Let's head out then." He kept his eyes steady on hers. "Do you need someone to ride with us?"

Rikki thought about it and slowly shook her head. "I think we're okay."

Ben felt his heart skip a beat. He loved the idea of her trusting him enough to take her home alone. He knew it would be nothing with another woman, but with Rikki, it was everything. Picking up her coat, he held it out for her, helping her into it. "Thanks for letting us come over," he said, his eyes on Marcus. It hadn't been easy for him to ask for what he needed, but Marcus had been kind about it.

"It's not a problem. Ever." Grace hugged Rikki. "You're welcome here anytime. You know that."

Rikki nodded. "I do. You admire my sister too much not to let me come over whenever I want."

Grace laughed. "That's very true!"

"I'm going to warm up my car. Give me a minute." He hurried out the door.

Rikki shrugged at Grace. "I'll probably turn into a statue

if I'm left in the cold too long. It's a good thing I've never been in cold weather before."

Marcus sighed. "He's being a gentleman. It's sad that you ladies haven't been around good men enough to recognize the quality."

Grace laughed and walked to Marcus, wrapping her arms around him. "I know what a gem you are. You don't have to keep reminding me."

As Rikki watched them, she wished she could have that ease with a man. She knew it wouldn't happen though. How could it? She couldn't ever trust anyone enough to put her arms around him so casually.

When Ben stepped back into the house, she turned to him, a sad look on her face. She'd have to tell him. How could she not? She wasn't about to let a nice man spend time thinking that she would ever be able to have a real relationship. That wouldn't be fair to either of them.

Ben saw the look on her face, and he knew she was going to tell him there was no future. He had a plan though. He wasn't about to let her get away with ending it now. No, she had to give him a fair shot, and he knew just how he was going to make sure she did it.

After they'd said their goodnights, Ben took Rikki's hand and led her out to his car. They'd have to talk it out tonight. He knew she wouldn't go out with him again otherwise.

3

Walking to Ben's car with him seemed more natural than Rikki had expected. He wasn't as scary as most men she knew. When they were both in and buckled, she grinned. "I think you're the only man in the area who doesn't drive a pick-up truck."

He grinned at her. "Wisconsin isn't as big into trucks as Wyoming seems to be. I like my car. We've been through good and bad times together."

"It seems nice."

"I'm glad you felt safe letting me drive you home," he said casually as he pulled into the driveway of Linda's house on the Culpepper Ranch.

Just like that her heartbeat sped up, and she felt the familiar fear. He was obviously not taking her somewhere other than home, though, so why did it hit then? "Maybe not completely safe, but I think I can honestly say I was willing to take the risk."

"And are you glad you did? Or are you freaking out now?"

Rikki laughed self-consciously. "Actually, I'm kind of

freaking out now. As soon as you said you were glad I trusted you, I started thinking you were going to do something evil to me. I know you're not, but my brain is messed up."

He sighed. "I'm not going to hurt you. I can't even kill bugs. I just take them outside where they belong."

"Wow. The perfect man. I never thought I'd find you." She made certain her voice sounded awestruck.

Ben laughed softly. "I'm anything but perfect. If I was perfect, I'd be visiting the bakery more to get to know you and not trying to force you to go out with me."

"Force me?" She raised an eyebrow, suddenly no longer nervous, and a little annoyed at his wording. "I'm past the days of letting a man force me into doing *anything*." She no longer did anything she didn't want to do—especially for a man!

Fascinated by her sudden show of strength, he put the car into park and turned to her, his hand stroking her cheek. "I didn't word that well. Maybe I should have paid more attention in my public speaking courses."

She couldn't help but grin at that. "I like you, Pastor Benjamin."

He groaned. "Please don't tell me you still think of me as Pastor Benjamin. I want to be just plain old Ben in your eyes."

She shrugged. "I guess you are. I was just messing around calling you that."

"Good." He looked into her eyes, his hand on her cheek shifting a bit and rubbing over her lips.

Rikki swallowed hard, her eyes going to his. *What's he thinking?*

"I don't want to scare you," he whispered softly, "but I'd really like to kiss you good night. May I?"

Her gaze dropped to his mouth as she nodded slowly. "I think so."

"You think so?" He couldn't help but laugh. "What an enthusiastic answer!"

She shrugged. "Well, I've never really been kissed. Just once when we were playing two minutes in a closet when I was eleven. Josh Williamson. I was sure I was going to grow up and have his babies, but his kiss was all wet and mushy, and I was done with him."

"No wet, mushy kisses. I'll keep that in mind."

"I don't think I'd mind if it was you."

Ben smiled. "Let's see." He slowly lowered his head toward hers, giving her every opportunity to back away if she was nervous. When she didn't, he brushed his lips across hers, careful to keep the kiss light.

When he pulled away, Rikki put her hand at the back of his neck, pulling him back down. Kissing him was nice! Much nicer than she'd imagined it would be.

"Do you want to go to the Christmas tree lighting in town with me on Saturday night?" he asked, his voice gruff.

"I don't really do well in crowds."

"Let's try it. If you get nervous, we can always leave. You won't be able to get back to doing things people consider normal if you don't try."

"You're being Pastor Benjamin again," she told him, wrinkling her nose. She definitely preferred Ben, who kissed her and made her tingle all over.

Ben sighed. "It's hard to separate them sometimes. Trust me, though. With you I'll always try to be Ben. Pastor Benjamin doesn't get to kiss the pretty girls. Only Ben gets to do that."

"Well then, I definitely prefer Ben!" She blushed as soon as the words left her mouth, realizing how forward she was being. It was true though. She did like kissing him. She leaned forward and rested her head on his shoulder for a moment. "I should go in. I don't want Linda to worry."

"How did you come to live here?" he asked, wanting just another few minutes with her. It was so hard to say goodnight.

"I was nervous about staying at my sister's house during her weeks in Texas, so Felicity Quinlan asked me to stay here. Then she married, and I still stayed here. Linda and I get along really well, and I don't think she likes living alone. Of course, I don't think she'll be alone much longer. She and Roy Williams are spending an awful lot of time together."

"Felicity seems like a whirlwind to me. I can't figure her out."

"Don't even try! It'll just hurt your head. I promise! Felicity is as sweet as can be, but she is pretty nuts."

Ben smiled. "I'd gotten that impression. She seems to be a good mom to her new step-son, though."

"Oh, she's wonderful. She just talks a mile a minute and confuses the living snot out of me."

"The living snot? I've never heard anyone say that before. How does snot live?"

"Sometimes it's best not to think about these things too hard. It just hurts."

Ben frowned at her. "I'm sensing a pattern here. You just refuse to think about things that are complicated or confusing, don't you?"

"It's just not good for my head. My kindergarten teacher got tired of my questions, so she started saying, 'Don't you worry your pretty little head about that.' So now I never worry about anything too confusing. It works for me."

"I can see it does." He kissed her once more, just as softly. "I'm going to walk you to your door."

Rikki smiled, opening her car door and getting out. "I had a really nice time. I'm glad we did this."

He smiled. "I am too. I'll come by around one tomorrow, and maybe we can have lunch together again?"

She nodded. "That sounds nice."

At the door, he touched her cheek briefly. "Sleep well, and dream of me."

Once she was inside, she leaned back against the door. How would she dream of anything else?

As soon as Rikki walked into the bakery the following morning, Grace pulled her off to the side. "How'd it go with Ben last night? Are you going to see him again?"

Rikki nodded. "I'm seeing him on Saturday, and he's supposed to come in for lunch around one today. Is it okay if I take my break with him?"

"Of course! Did he kiss you?"

"You're not supposed to ask me that! Ladies don't kiss and tell!"

"Sure, they do! Gentlemen don't, but ladies do it all the time. So?"

Rikki noticed that Patience and Felicity were making no secret of the fact they were both listening as well. "Maybe we should get some baking done today. Isn't there a baby shower this weekend?"

Grace wrinkled her nose. "Yeah, yeah, yeah. Work always has to come first. When I have a baby, I'm making my own cake, and it's going to be gorgeous!"

"Are you telling us something?" Patience asked, eyeing Grace's slender figure.

Grace made a face at her cousin. "No, and if I was, I'd find a better way to do it. We're waiting a while before we have munchkins. There are enough little Quinlans on the way."

"Probably. But we don't have any bakery babies." Felicity sighed dramatically. "Who will my baby play with?" She wasn't showing yet, but she liked to practice the pregnant waddle, because it made her feel special.

"Maybe Rikki will have one," Grace suggested.

Rikki shook her head vehemently. "No way. I'm not getting married right away. I'm not like you guys."

Grace gave Felicity and Patience a knowing look and got back to work, while Rikki went to handle the person who'd just walked into the bakery.

When Ben arrived for lunch, he brought with him a picnic basket. Rikki raised an eyebrow at him. "You do know we sell food here."

"I know. I ate some yesterday. I happened to mention to Lovie that I was coming here for lunch and then next thing I knew, I had this picnic basket in my hands. She said I should buy us drinks here."

Rikki shrugged. "Okay. What do you want?"

"Coffee. This girl I know kept me out way too late last night. She wore me out!"

"Oh, and you had nothing to do with it? You weren't a willing participant in the staying out lateness?"

Ben shook his head seriously. "Of course not. How could I be? I'm a pastor after all."

"A pastor who has no respect for tomorrow, maybe?"

"How could I when I'm sitting with a pretty girl?"

Rikki shook her head at him, getting his coffee and grabbing a bottle of water for herself. Looking over her shoulder, she saw all three of her co-workers watching her intently.

Not one of them even tried to hide it. "I'm taking my lunch break!"

Felicity sighed dramatically. "I told you we needed cameras installed in the dining area."

Rikki shook her head when Ben gave her a confused look. "Ignore them. All three of them are absolutely insane. If you listen to them, it just humors them, and they get even more outrageous."

"So, I should pretend I didn't hear them at all?"

"It's the only course of action that will have a good outcome. I promise you this!" She loved her co-workers, but they were all insane. Every single one of them.

He set the picnic basket in the middle of a large table and together they unloaded it. "Fried chicken? She made us fried chicken for a lunch date in the middle of the day in an establishment that serves food?" Rikki shook her head. There was something about Lovie that was almost as strange as Brother Anthony.

"I guess so. I hadn't peeked yet. What else is in here?" He pulled a large container of potato salad and another of baked beans out of the basket. "I guess we're having a traditional picnic feast."

Rikki laughed. "It's a good thing we don't have any other customers right now. They'd all start expecting picnic fixings to be sold here, and we just don't have the manpower." She pulled a sheet of paper from the bottom, and read the note aloud. "Since you're having lunch in a bakery, go ahead and buy some brownies for dessert. I didn't have time to bake."

He shook his head at her, sitting down at the table. "Thanks for having lunch with me."

"You didn't exactly give me a choice. You announced we were doing this."

"Well, you didn't kick me and run away screaming, so I guess we're good, right?"

She shrugged. "I guess so." Taking the seat opposite him, she put some of the chicken on a paper plate from the basket. "She thought of everything, didn't she?"

"Lovie is a pretty organized woman. She always thinks of everything." He leaned forward a little. "To tell you the truth, she kind of scares me."

Rikki laughed. "Why is she scary?"

"Well, she does this pageant with the kids for Christmas every year, and this year, she announced that it was time for younger blood to take over, and it was all mine. I've been looking at her notes, and she has songs, a living nativity, and there's this cute little play about what Christmas means. I haven't even started auditioning kids yet!"

She frowned. "We only have about four weeks 'til Christmas. When is the pageant?"

"Christmas Eve. It's part of the church's celebration of the holiday."

"Do you need some help? I've never done a Christmas pageant, but I did some theater in school. Don't tell anyone, because people think I want to be just like Valerie when I admit it, but I do love working behind the scenes on plays."

Ben didn't need to hear her offer twice. It would give them more time together, and he could really use the help. "I would love your help! Auditions are tonight. Can you be there?"

Rikki frowned. "Did you just con me into helping you with this thing?"

"Con you? How can I con someone who volunteered?"

"Pastors always know the right way to ask for something without ever asking. Yeah, I can be there. I think. What time?"

"Auditions start at seven."

She nodded slowly. "I get out of here at six, so I can be there by six thirty or so. If I don't eat first."

"I'll get something from Bob's Burger Barn and meet you at the church. Will that work?"

"Are we allowed to eat in the church?" she asked, feeling very skeptical. How could he even suggest eating in the church, when Brother Anthony and Lovie would probably be livid?

He shrugged. "No one told me I couldn't, and it's the only way you'll be able to eat tonight. We'll spread a table cloth under our chairs."

Rikki reached out and covered his hand with hers, still amazed at the size difference. He made her feel puny...and protected. "I'll be there."

Ben grinned at her, his face lighting up. "Thank you so much! I'm sure it'll be the best pageant this town has ever seen!"

She sighed as she took a bite of her beans. "I sure hope so. I'm a little worried that people will expect more from us than we can possibly deliver."

"Rising up to other's expectations can show us how strong we really are."

"I used to be strong." Her voice was soft, barely a whisper, but he heard it.

"You're stronger than you think you are. Think about it, Rikki. We were alone in my car last night for twenty minutes. You didn't once start screaming and begging me to let you out."

She chuckled. "I bet that's something you've never said to another woman after a first date." And the fact that he'd considered he might have to say it to her showed just how messed up in the head she really was.

"I've never known another woman who's had to be as strong as you have. You amaze me. You went through something very few people could have survived with their spirit intact, and now you're dealing with the aftermath. A lot of people would have just refused to go on. You're not only going on, you're building a new life for yourself!"

She nodded. "I'm surprised you haven't asked more about what happened. Did you read all the online stuff about it?"

"I did read a lot of it. Not all. I know you were taken from your hometown and driven from Iowa to Texas where you were held in exchange for your sister."

She took a sip of her water, watching him. "The articles don't tell you that he took me from my job. I was just getting off work at the only grocery store in town. I went out to my car, and Curtis was standing there, leaning against the hood. He told me how upset he was that my sister had broken up with him, and he asked me to go for a cup of coffee with him, so we could talk. I felt so bad for him, because he and Valerie had been together for eight years, and the very day they broke up, she married Jesse." She shook her head. "I really can't believe how stupid I was."

"That sounds like you were caring. Not stupid. How long did it take you to realize he was keeping you hostage?"

"He drove me straight out of town. As soon as we hit the countryside, I told him to pull over. I knew I could walk back to town, and all would be fine. Instead he used some duct tape, and he 'tied' my hands together, and he put a piece over my mouth, so I couldn't talk. He kept me like that except for letting me out to use the bathroom every few hours for two days. I didn't get any food. He'd give me a sip of water, and then re-tape my mouth."

"How'd you get away?" He'd read about her sister taking her place, but he knew she needed to talk about it.

"He didn't want me. He only wanted Valerie. They were so awful together, but all he could see was that the woman he loved was married to another man. So, he did whatever it took to get her back. When we got to Wiggieville, where the set is, he called her from my phone. He told her where we were and to come with no help. So, she did. She came right there to take my place with no questions asked. Do you have any idea how guilty that made me feel? I've always been so jealous of her. It annoyed me when people compared us, and there she was willing to put her life on the line for mine."

"You didn't know she'd do that."

"Of course I did! She's always been my protector. The person who loved me even when I didn't deserve it. I wasn't always kind to her either. I'd yell at her and tell her she was ruining my life by being famous." Rikki shook her head, ashamed to admit what a brat she'd been. "I was even mad at her for marrying Jesse. I had a crush on him from the very first episode of *Lazy Love*."

"It sounds like you don't feel that way anymore," he said. It was hard for him to find the line between friend and counselor as she talked to him about what had happened, but he knew she needed to tell him everything. She couldn't just let him believe what he'd read online.

"I don't feel that way anymore. I watched my sister put her life on the line for me. She walked to me, whispered to me where to find Jesse who would help me, and then she watched me leave. She became his prisoner for me."

"How did she get away? None of the articles mentioned that part."

"They knew I was missing, so she insisted Jesse teach

her to shoot. The gun was still in the car. She and Jesse were having dinner in town, and she went to the car, got the gun, and ran to the hotel where Curtis was keeping me. As soon as I left, she threatened him with the gun, but he didn't listen. He told her she'd never be able to shoot him. He didn't know how much stronger she was with Jesse." She shook her head. "That's when I found out Curtis had been beating her for years. He'd always been verbally abusive, but when she started working with Jesse he became physically abusive as well. So, she not only saved me, she did so by putting herself in the hands of a man who she knew would hurt her."

"Wow."

"Yeah. She shot him in the shoulder. I found Jesse and told him everything, and he rushed to save her. She was waiting for him calmly. My sister is something else."

Ben couldn't help but agree with her. "I've only met her once or twice, but she doesn't seem like someone who could shoot anyone."

Rikki nodded, swiping at a tear. She'd thought she was out of tears about that particular situation, but here they were all over again. "And then when I was messed up in the head, and I didn't want to go on anti-depressants, she offered me a place to live here. She said I could be her nanny the one week out of the month she lives here instead of in Texas." She shook her head. "She won't use a nanny. I knew it at the time. It's not who she is. She'll have one while she's on the set, but here in Wyoming, that baby will be with her all the time."

"So, why'd you come? Did you know that when you agreed?"

"Yeah, but I needed to get out of town. Everywhere I looked I was reminded of what happened. In my house, with my mom, all I could think about was what a brat I'd been, putting myself in danger that way. I'd been warned he might be after us! Do you want to know what I was thinking when I got into that van with Curtis?"

Ben wasn't sure he did want to know, but he nodded. "Sure."

"I thought if I could work with Curtis to split them up, maybe I'd have a chance with Jesse after all. Can you believe that?"

"That doesn't make the kidnapping your fault. And I think you've grown from it."

She laughed derisively. "Yeah. I've grown into a phobic nincompoop."

"I wouldn't say that at all."

"Wait 'til you get to know me a little better. Then you'll agree wholeheartedly."

4

Rikki got to the church just on time. She'd hurried home to change, and had worried she wouldn't make it. As soon as she walked into the church, she found a small crowd of people, and she felt her heart leap into her throat. She took deep breaths, trying to fend off the panic attack. There was nothing worrisome about these people. She knew all of them individually, but the crowd made her nervous.

She wasn't certain why she was afraid of crowds. It didn't make sense to her, but every time she was in one, she started to freak out the same way she did when she got out of her car, and the same way she did in an enclosed space.

Her eyes searched through the people, and she found Ben, standing amidst them all. He held a hand out in her direction, and she hurried toward him, taking it and holding on tight. Immediately her breathing calmed. She said nothing, but she tilted her head a tiny bit, resting it against his shoulder. She needed him.

He looked down at her with a smile, answering a question from Mrs. Pfaffenbach, who was trying to make sure no peanut butter would be served in the building while her son, allergic to peanuts, was there. When he assured her they would be careful of peanuts, which were banned from the church due to her son's allergies, she smiled and nodded. "I'll be back in an hour. You did say that we should plan on leaving them an hour."

"At *least* an hour. I'm not sure how long the auditions will take. Rikki Dobson is going to help me with them, but there are a lot of kids and a lot of parts."

Mrs. Pfaffenbach frowned. "I'll be back for little Timmy soon. Try to have the boys audition first, so he's not late going to bed."

Rikki smiled sweetly. "Mrs. Pfaffenbach, every one of these children will need to go to bed at a decent hour. We'll do our best to get them all out on time, but the sooner we get started, the sooner we'll be done. Thank you for letting Timmy audition."

Ben bit his lip. Rikki wasn't an employee of the church, so she could more easily say what was on her mind. He had to constantly worry that he would lose his job if he was *too* direct.

"I'll be back!" Mrs. Pfaffenbach spun on her heel and hurried toward the door. She was obviously annoyed, but no one ever spoke up against Rikki. They were all worried she was too fragile.

Rikki stood on tiptoe to whisper, "You're welcome!"

Ben fought back a laugh. She really had helped him with her comments to the silly woman. He understood the food allergy, but if Timmy was going to be part of the pageant, there would be some nights where he would stay up past eight. It was just going to happen.

He looked around, raising his voice to be heard. "I want all the boys on the right side of the sanctuary, and all the girls on the left. We're going to have you sing a little song and read some lines."

As the children filed to sit where they'd been told, he took Rikki's hand. "I've got burgers under the seat in third row center. There's a root beer for you there too."

She frowned at him. "There's nothing online that talks about my obsession with root beer. How'd you know?"

He grinned. "Grace tells lots of stuff."

Rikki shook her head. "That Grace…"

"But I knew your favorite drink. That's a good thing, right?"

"Just so she's not telling all my deepest darkest secrets…" She'd told him them all herself that day. She hadn't once mentioned her guilt in the kidnapping to anyone but him. She couldn't help but wonder if it had been wise to be so honest about it.

As soon as they were sitting, she divvied up the burgers, carefully peeling the pickle off hers. "I hate pickles," she whispered.

"Why?"

"I don't know! They're just gross, and their juice gets all over everything." She took a big bite of the burger, trying not to grimace at the pickle juice on her bun. "Thanks for getting dinner for us."

He popped a fry into his mouth. "Thanks for helping me with this pageant. I'm more than a little overwhelmed. Does it bother you?"

She shrugged. "When I first walked into the church and saw everyone here, I started to panic, but when you held your hand out for me, it helped. You're going to be my port in the storm."

"I'd be happy to be your port in the storm. I'd be happy to be yours. Period."

Rikki looked at him questioningly. "What are you trying to say, Pastor Benjamin?"

"I'm trying to say that I think you're pretty terrific, and I want to be your steady Eddie."

"My steady Eddie? Really?"

"Sure. What do you say, Betty?"

"Do we have to call each other Eddie and Betty?"

He shrugged. "I guess you could call me Freddy!"

She shook her head. "I guess you can't be my steady Eddie then."

"Fine. You can call me Ben, and I'll call you Veronica."

"Try again! No one calls me Veronica except my doctor."

"Rikki then. You sure you aren't willing to have fun with names?" Ben asked.

She nodded. "Positive. Ben and Rikki works for me."

"So, you'll let me be your steady Ben?" He'd made a joke of it, but he wanted to make sure she saw no other men, and wasn't sure how to phrase it otherwise.

"Yeah." She couldn't look at him as she said it, way too embarrassed. And there was no way she could see herself with anyone else.

He stood up and asked a couple of the children to go on stage and sing a song of their choice. Once he was seated again, he looked at her. "You said earlier you had a crush on your sister's husband, Jesse. Do you still?"

She shook her head, hiding her laughter. "Absolutely not! The first time I sat down with him and talked to him, I knew he belonged with Valerie. He's had feelings for her since the moment they met."

"And that stopped your feelings?"

"He's not the person he is on TV. I think I was in love with Dr. Dylan, not with Jesse Savoy. He and Valerie really are a perfect fit. I'm glad he's making my sister happy, but I wouldn't have him on a bet."

"I'm glad to hear that. And you're not in love with any other big stars right? Your heart is wide open for me?"

"I don't know about that. I'm not in love with anyone else, but my heart has felt a bit closed off lately."

"I'll help you fix that!"

Two children, a boy and a girl stepped onto the stage, singing together. "Those two are Noah and Hailey. They're brother and sister," he whispered. "They always get the leads."

"Why do they always get the leads?" she asked, surprised that the same kids got it year after year.

"They have the best voices I hear." He sighed. "I want to give new kids a chance to do it."

The pair on the stage broke into a slightly off-key rendition of *Away in a Manger*. It wasn't bad, but it certainly wasn't wonderful. Ben made a note on his clipboard as they left the stage.

"There has to be someone better than those two," Rikki whispered.

"We'll do our best."

The next child to go up on stage was Corinne, Patience's new step-daughter, whom Rikki knew well. She sang *Jingle Bells* complete with her own dance that was beautifully choreographed. "Is there a dance part?" Rikki asked.

"There is now," he responded. "There's no way we can let that child's talent go to waste." He grinned as she danced around the stage to her own terrible rendition of the song. "Remind me not to let her sing, though."

Two hours later, they'd seen everyone, and brought a couple of the children onto the stage a second time. Ben stood. "Thanks, we'll start rehearsals on Friday night. I'll send an email out on Thursday with everyone's part." They already knew everyone would have to have a part, and they were simply figuring out which roles they would each have.

The children hurried to their mothers, and Rikki waved at Patience, who picked up a sleepy Corinne.

When the church was empty except for the two of them, Rikki sagged in her chair. "That was a lot more work than I thought it would be."

"And there were two of us! Imagine how bad it would have been with only one person."

"I don't even want to think about it." Rikki stifled a yawn. "Do we hash out their parts tonight? Or work on that tomorrow?"

"Why don't I come to your place tomorrow. We can work on it there."

"Sure," Rikki responded. "Linda won't mind. I'll even cook dinner."

"You're going to feed me? May I get down on my knees and kiss your feet now, or should I wait until tomorrow?"

Rikki laughed. "Maybe you should wait and see if the cooking is worth the foot kissing. I've cooked some, but I'm not a gourmet by any means."

"I have been cooking for myself and eating out since I got to Culpepper. Occasionally Lovie and Brother Anthony will have me over for a meal, but usually I'm on my own. I'm looking forward to eating something different."

"I'm just going to make a casserole." She'd already thought about something she could make quickly. "Why don't you come by around seven or seven fifteen? I can have it ready by then."

He nodded. "Sounds good. I made notes on all the kids, so we should be able to remember who did what."

"Promise we'll find a way for Corinne to dance?"

"How could we not? She was made to dance!"

Rikki got to her feet. "I need to get home if I'm going to get enough sleep to make it through tomorrow. I enjoy being with you, but you're sure cutting down on my sleep time."

He stood, walking with her toward the door. "I'm going to walk you to your car."

"I appreciate it."

"I'm not doing it for you. I think we need to have a goodnight kiss as close to saying goodbye for the night as possible. It's essential to our moving forward as a couple."

"Are we a couple?" she asked, surprised at how much she liked the idea.

"Yup. If I'm going to be your steady Eddie, then we're a couple. It's just how it works."

"I thought we decided on steady Ben?"

"Fine, steady Ben. Do you know how much less fun that sounds?"

He stopped to lock the church building and walked her to her car, waiting while she unlocked the door. "I should have picked you up."

"Wouldn't have worked! The moms and kids would have been breaking down the door of the church waiting for you."

"Probably, which is why I didn't. I wish I was driving you home, though."

She smiled, reaching out and putting her palm flat on his chest. "I wish you were too, but I'll be fine. I'll call my sister as I leave, and she'll talk to me the whole way home."

"I hope you have hands-free."

"I do. I'll be fine. I promise."

He leaned down and brushed her lips with his. "So, I'll see you tomorrow night?"

"Seven. My place." She stepped closer to him, wrapping

her arms around his neck. "Your kisses are lots better than Josh Williamson's."

"You need to quit comparing me to your first love. I'll have to hunt him down."

She laughed. "I doubt if he even remembers my name."

"Oh, trust me. He does. I'm sure he's been pining away for you since your time together in that closet. No more time in closets with anyone but me!"

"I don't spend time in closets even alone anymore. Too scary."

He sighed. "I'm sorry I made you remember it."

"Actually, the more time I spend with you, the more distant it all seems. I'm doing okay."

"I'm glad." He pressed his lips to hers, his hand going under her hair in the back, stroking her neck.

Rikki shuddered, her lips parting for his.

He raised his head. "Did I scare you?"

She shook her head. It had been exactly the opposite. She'd shuddered because what he'd done to her had felt so deliciously good. After living in an emotional vacuum for eight months, it felt good to be touched and to enjoy it for a change. "I like it when you kiss me."

"You keep thinking that. I'll be dragging you off to the altar before too terribly long, you know. We've been dating for two whole days. In Culpepper that's equivalent to eight years somewhere else."

"I don't know about the altar yet, but I sure enjoy being with you. Thanks for reminding me that I can smile and laugh."

With one last kiss, he opened her car door for her. "I'll see you tomorrow night." As she drove off, he stared after the car. He'd never felt so much after such a short time dating a girl. She was his future. He knew it with everything inside him. Now he just had to convince her.

―――

BEN SURPRISED Rikki at work the next day with a bouquet of flowers. "Do you want to have lunch with me?"

Rikki smiled and nodded. She turned to the three women who were watching her so intently. "Any objections to me having lunch with Ben?"

Grace shook her head, the spokeswoman for the three of them as usual. "Not at all. Enjoy yourselves."

Rikki picked out a few things for the two of them from the display, making a note to pay later. "Lunch is on me today," she told him.

"You can't buy me lunch!"

"Why not? You've bought me lunch. And dinner. Why can't I buy for you?"

"I don't know! It's just supposed to be the man buying lunch. Not the drop-dead gorgeous woman he's dating."

She rolled her eyes, grabbing a coffee for him and a bottle of water for herself, before putting everything on a tray. "I'm not that old-fashioned."

He picked up the tray, carrying it toward the dining area. "I am. This may cause problems. How do you feel about men opening doors for you and buying engagement rings?"

It was the second time he'd mentioned marriage in a couple of days, and she was getting a bit nervous. "I think it's fine if men do both things if they want to. But if they feel obligated to do it, then it's not nearly as much fun!"

He grinned. "Fine. I'll do my best not to feel obligated to do anything." He set the tray on the table and took a seat. "Thanks for lunch."

"You're very welcome." Rikki dug through the bag, finding kolaches for both of them. It was the only think they served that had a decent amount of protein in it. "So, what brings you out to the Culpepper Ranch today?" she asked.

"What else? The most beautiful woman in all of Wyoming."

"Only because my sister's in Texas."

"When will she be back? Isn't it about time?"

She shook her head. "She's too far along to fly, so she's staying in Texas until after the baby is born. I hate it, but she doesn't really have a choice."

"When is she due?"

"Mid-January. I'm so ready for her to be back to her normal self. And I'm ready to have a little nephew to love."

"It's a boy? Is that public information?"

"Nope. They didn't think anyone should know it but them."

"Do they have a name yet?"

Rikki shook her head. "They're waiting to make that announcement. The girl who plays Valerie's sister on Lazy Love thinks they should name the baby after her. She's determined that Amber is a fine name for a boy."

He laughed. "They're not going to go for that, are they?"

"Nope. Jesse will make sure they name him something manly." She eyed him as she took a gulp of water from her bottle. "You don't have to drive out here for lunch every day, you know."

"I know. I just like to spend time with you."

"I like it too. It just seems odd that we went from casual acquaintances to seeing each other twice a day so quickly." Not that she was complaining. At all. She loved every moment she got to spend with him.

"You've heard how quickly everyone marries in Culpepper, haven't you? It's like this strange phenomenon."

"I've seen some of it happen, so yes, I know about it. I just don't think it would work for me. How can I trust a man enough to marry him on a short acquaintance? Why, I'm sure I'd need to know a man for at least a week," she said with a wink.

He laughed. "Well, technically we met in August so we've known each other for a few months. We should get married quickly, before Brother Anthony finds out!"

She shook her head, laughing. "I think maybe we should wait a little longer. Like at least a week or two."

"I'm not so sure about that. Maybe another twenty-four hours or so."

"I'm not going to let you rush me into doing something I don't want to do, Pastor Benjamin!"

"You know you only call me that when you're scolding me about something? I'm not sure I like it."

She shrugged. "It's your name!"

"I like the way you say Ben better. It sounds nice on your lips. Almost as nice as my lips feel on them."

"You're really in a mood today!"

"I woke up and you were my first thought. I couldn't wait to see you. I almost called you this morning just so I could hear your voice. I'm falling in love with you, Rikki Dobson, and I'm going to make sure you know it every minute of every day."

Her eyes grew wide as she stared at him. "What do they put in the water around here to make everyone's feelings so accelerated?"

"Everyone's? Does that mean you're starting to have feelings too?"

She blushed. "I wouldn't be dating you if I didn't. I wasn't sure I'd ever feel comfortable with a man again, and in a situation where I was already frightened, you calmed me down. How weird is that? Yes, I'm starting to have feelings for you. Strong feelings."

"You should think about marrying me then. What do we have to lose?"

"Our minds?"

He grinned at that. "I'm not going to touch you without being married to you. Not really. Quick kisses are one thing, but not only am I a pastor with a reputation to uphold, but I'm also a man who believes in purity until marriage. So... you should marry me. Then we don't have to worry about any of that nonsense."

She sighed. "You need to be sure of what you feel before I can agree to marry you. We'll spend more time together. We'll see whether or not we're a good team as we work on this pageant together. Speaking of which, do you have any idea who you want to cast as the two main singers?" The pageant had three things going on at once, so most every child got a part. Some would play in the living nativity. Some would sing. And some would act out the play. In the past, the best singers had also been the stars of the play, but they'd decided it would be better to have more children with bigger roles. It would keep everyone happy.

"I know who is going to dance while the others sing. I haven't gotten a lot further than that."

"I really liked little Sara Samuels voice for the female lead singer. And maybe Byron Lane as the male voice."

He thought about it for a moment. "They're both so young, but they do have the best voices. If all they have to learn are the songs, I think they could handle it."

"That's settled then. Didn't you say you have CDs of the songs they need to learn?"

"I do. I'll send one home with each child on Friday. I'm sure Mrs. Peot, Noah and Hailey's mother will be furious with us, but things need to be shaken up around here."

"And we're just the people to do it!" She loved that she already felt like they were a team, working on the same side. If he could deal with her when she had her panic attacks, then she was sure they would be a match made in heaven. So far, he hadn't disappointed her at all.

5

When she rushed in the door after work, Rikki realized she hadn't really talked to Linda in a couple of days which was odd for her. Usually they would sit and talk for at least a few minutes every day, but she'd been so busy lately.

Linda was in nice slacks and a pretty blouse when Rikki hurried into the kitchen to start dinner. "Are you going out tonight?"

"Yeah. Roy needs to make sure the Christmas lights are ready for the celebration Saturday night, and he promised me dinner and dancing after. It'll probably be dinner at the diner and dancing at the Culpepper Watering Hole, but I'll take it. It's more about spending time with him than anything."

"So, you're going with him to check on the Christmas lights? It sounds like things are getting serious!"

Linda shrugged, her face turning red. "Maybe a little. Roy's a good man."

"He is!" Rikki pulled some ground beef out of the freezer to thaw in the microwave. "Speaking of good men...Ben is coming over for supper, and we're going to talk about casting for the Christmas pageant at church."

"I love the church's Christmas pageant. The kids do the funniest things. Last year little Robbie Becker stood in the middle of the stage for a solo, and he picked his nose instead."

Rikki laughed while making a mental note to remind the children that picking their noses on stage was not acceptable. "I hope we don't have any nose pickers this year!"

"There's always something! One year one of the children fell off the stage. Another one of the kids forgot the words to *Away in a Manger*, so he sang *Baby Got Back* instead. You should have seen Brother Anthony's face with that one!"

Rikki shook her head, laughing as she pictured the scene. "I'll have to warn Ben to expect those things. I'm not sure he knows they're in the realm of possibilities."

"The thing you need to know about working with children—and especially little boys—is to expect the unexpected. If they don't do something silly, you won't know it's real."

"I like that. I'll tell Ben you said so." Rikki got the meat out of the microwave and pulled out a pan to brown it in.

"I'm really glad you gave Pastor Benjamin a chance. You've smiled and laughed more in the past ten minutes than I've seen since you moved in here. I think he's good for you." The doorbell rang, and Linda pulled on her coat. "I'll see you soon. I hope." She hugged Rikki and hurried to the door.

After Linda left, Rikki mulled over what she'd said. She really was smiling and laughing more, though she hadn't realized it. For months she'd been so focused on just getting by that she'd missed out. It was almost like she was waking up from a foggy nightmare.

While she chopped tomatoes for a salad, she decided it was time she took control of her life. Yes, she'd had something terrible happen to her, but she didn't need to dwell on it forever. She could live her life to the fullest, and be happy, no matter what had happened.

Sure, she'd still be afraid of some things that others saw as normal, but she didn't have to live in her nightmare world forever. It was time for her to spread her wings, and if that meant giving the sweet man who was dating her a chance, then that's exactly what she'd do!

While the casserole was in the oven, she hurried to her room and changed into something clean. She'd never thought about just how messy it would be to work around flour and sugar all day, but though she did little of the baking, she did do her share of the frosting when the other ladies' hands got sore. She always seemed to be covered in something white.

She was just coming out of her bedroom in a pair of jeans and a pink sweater when the doorbell rang, and she hurried to open the door. Ben was leaning against the doorjamb, looking more adorable than ever. It was snowing, and he was wearing a cowboy hat. Just one look at him had her knees turning to mush. "Come in! Dinner will be ready in a few minutes. I have salad ready now if you're starving, or I could just serve it with the meal." She was nervous, which surprised her. They'd spent a lot of time together lately, and she hadn't expected the skittish feeling.

Ben stepped into the house and shut the door behind him, looking around. "Where's Mrs. Culpepper?"

"She's out with Roy. Something about making sure the Christmas lights were in working order for the lighting ceremony on Saturday, and then dinner and dancing."

Ben caught her by the waist and pulled her to him.

"Good. Then I don't have to worry about anyone walking in on us when I kiss you."

Rikki grinned up at him, before wrapping her arms around his neck. "Show me what you've got."

He chuckled, lowering his lips to hers. "It's hard to kiss you when I'm laughing, you know."

"So, stop laughing and get serious about the kissing!" She pressed her lips to his, stroking his shoulders through his thick jacket. When it occurred to her she wanted his clothes off, she took a step back. "On second thought, maybe I should set the table."

He grabbed her hand, a concerned look on his face. "What's wrong? I didn't scare you, did I?"

She shook her head. "Not scared at all."

"Then tell me what's wrong!" he insisted. It was hard to know how to handle her with her history, but he wanted to understand what she needed at all times.

"I was just thinking about how much I'd like it if we could get your clothes off, and I could feel bare skin. I didn't think that was an appropriate thought to have with the pastor I'm dating, so I thought I should step away for a bit instead."

His eyes widened, and a grin slowly formed. "I don't think it's an appropriate thought, but I like that you had it."

She made a face, turned on her heel, and returned to the kitchen. She wasn't going to discuss it with him any more than she already had. He was pleased with her thinking carnal thoughts, and that just wasn't right.

Ben removed his coat and threw it over the back of the couch before joining her in the kitchen. "How can I help?"

She took some glasses out of the cabinet. "Get us drinks."

"What should I get?"

Rikki shrugged. "I don't know. Dig through the fridge and figure it out."

She got down plates and salad bowls, hurrying around the counter and away from him. The kitchen was too small for her to share it with him. Linda was always calling it a one-butt kitchen.

Once they were sitting down to eat, she brought up the topic he was there to discuss. "I forgot my notes in the car. We can talk about it after dinner."

Rikki frowned. "I don't know that you should stay after dinner. I'm starting to think I can't be trusted alone with you."

He laughed. "Sure, you can. I'm strong. I'll fend you off."

"Whatever." She forked up a bite of her food.

"For what it's worth, I'm glad I'm not the only one having those kinds of thoughts."

Her eyes met his. "You are too?"

"I'm a pastor, but I'm still a man, and you're a very beautiful woman. That's why we should get married."

"Married, huh? If I agreed, you'd run screaming into the night."

"Try me." His eyes met hers steadily. There was nothing he wanted more at that moment than her agreement.

"I can't marry you! I don't even know where you live!"

"I have a small apartment in town. Next question."

Rikki shook her head. "No. It's too soon."

"Why is it too soon? Is it too soon because you're afraid of me? Or because you're afraid of your feelings for me?"

She didn't answer him, but they both knew what her problem was. She felt too much for him, and after spending so much time with her feelings put on hold, she wasn't sure how to handle them. "I think we should change the subject."

He caught her hand and brought it to his lips. "Promise

me you'll think about it. I feel so much for you. I don't want to go on this way."

She sighed. "I'll think about it. I don't want to rush into anything though. I feel like I'm waking up from a really long nightmare, and it would be easy to jump into something I'm not ready for right now, and I don't want that to happen."

He nodded. "I don't want to force you into anything, but I do think we'd be really good together."

After supper, he ran to his car to get the notes he'd taken while she loaded the dishwasher, her mind on nothing but what he was asking her. Constantly he brought up the subject of marriage, and deep inside her, she knew it was what she wanted. But what if it was just a gut reaction? What if she just wanted to be with someone who would protect her? She had to be sure.

They sat together on the couch, with him reading the notes he'd made on each of the children, while she wrote down what part they'd assigned each of them. It was a long process given that over forty children had auditioned.

Finally, she'd written the last name next to the role they'd assigned the child. "That's it. We're done."

He grinned, rubbing the back of his neck. "Are you sure it's going to be all right to have Corinne choreograph her own dance? She won't do anything inappropriate, will she?"

"Absolutely not! There will be a lot of spinning and leaps, but nothing that could even begin to be considered inappropriate."

"Okay, then she's in." He put all the papers on the couch beside him, before scooting closer to her. "I need to leave soon."

"I hate it when you leave."

"That's another reason you should marry me. We won't have to part at night. You could sleep in my arms."

"I would have no complaints about that." She snuggled close, resting her head on his shoulder. "I told my sister a little about you last night. She wants to meet you."

"To make sure I'm good enough for her sister?" he asked, frowning.

"Nope. She wants to thank the man who taught me to laugh again. Jesse will want to make sure you're good enough."

He kissed the top of her head. "We should fly down and see them then."

"Fly to Texas? Are you crazy?"

"What's so crazy about it? She can't come here, and we're perfectly mobile. Why not?"

"Do you really think it would be okay to travel together without being married?"

He shrugged. "As long as we didn't share a bed, I don't see why not. We could fly down on Sunday and come back Tuesday."

She looked at him for a minute before slowly nodding. Getting Valerie and Jesse's opinion of him would help her a lot. And she wanted to see Amber, of course. She liked to think of Amber as her sister, because Amber played Valerie's sister on TV. "If you're really willing, let's do it!"

"See if your sister would mind!"

Rikki dug her phone from her pocket and checked the time before calling. It was almost ten in Texas, but Valerie should still be up. She called using Facetime, like she always did, preferring to see her sister while she talked to her.

"Hey, you!" Valerie said when she answered.

"Hi! When's your next break in filming?"

"Next week. Why? Are you coming to see me?" Valerie asked.

Jesse stuck his head between Valerie and the screen.

"Hey, Rikki! Valerie is starting to waddle when she walks. It's so cute!"

Rikki giggled softly. "Valerie, this is Ben. I think you guys have met a couple of times."

"Hi, Pastor Benjamin. Rikki has said some nice things about you."

"She speaks very highly of you as well!" Ben responded.

Rikki shook her head. "No more mutual admiration society for now. How would it be if Ben and I flew down on Sunday afternoon and came back Tuesday? It would be a short trip, but I really want you two to get to know each other better. I need to clear it with Grace, but I don't think it'll be a problem. She's been urging me to take a few days off."

Valerie nodded excitedly. "I'd love that! I feel like it's been forever since I hugged my little sister."

"It's been less than a month."

"So? It still feels like forever. Call Grace, and text me her answer. If it's yes, I'll get your plane tickets. I don't want you to have to spend your hard-earned money just to see me."

"So, I can spend yours instead?"

"I do make a little more than you do."

Rikki nodded reluctantly. "All right. I'll text you in a few." She tapped her screen to end the call, and immediately called Grace.

"Hello?"

"Grace, you know how you've been trying to get me to take a couple of days off?"

"Yeah…"

"How about Monday and Tuesday? Ben and I are thinking about flying down to see Valerie and Jesse."

"Seriously?" Grace asked.

"Yeah, seriously. Would that be a problem?"

"Not at all! Go for it. If we get too busy, I can drag one of my sisters in."

"I guess that's the benefit of having five sisters, huh?"

"There has to be one somewhere!"

Rikki laughed. "Thanks, Grace. I'll see you in the morning." Without pause, she ended the call and quickly texted her sister. *All good. We'll see you Sunday.*

Tickets purchased. I had all the information typed in and just had to push the final button.

Aren't you clever?

Of course, I am. I picked you to be my baby sister.

You picked me? *Was I in a field of babies and you chose the one you wanted?*

Something like that. We'll pick you up at the airport on Sunday. Love you bunches!

Love you! Rikki turned to Ben. "It's all set."

"Wow. That was quick."

"Are you having second thoughts?"

He put his index finger under her chin and tilted her face up for his kiss. "How could I have second thoughts? If this will make you feel better about me, then I'm all for it."

She heard a ding, and looked down at her phone again. There was an email from Valerie with the flight information. "We fly out at four. Does that work?"

"Sure. Are they picking us up at the airport, or do we need to rent a car?"

"She said they'd pick us up. Since they're not filming next week, it's easy for them to get away."

"Okay, that sounds good. I'm going to email all the mothers of the children about their parts in the pageant. We rehearse on Friday night, go to the tree lighting on Saturday, fly to Texas on Sunday, come back on Tuesday, and rehearsals start on Wednesday. We're going to be too tired to think."

She grinned. "Maybe that will make it easier for me not to picture you in less clothes."

"I'd offer to send you a shirtless picture, but it would be inappropriate. My mother always claimed that men running around with no shirts on were too broke to buy them, and she told me if I ever got that broke, I needed to ask her for money."

Rikki laughed. "She sounds like an interesting woman. I need to meet her someday."

"Someday you will. Probably not this month, though. She's pretty busy."

"What does she do?"

"She's a nurse at a hospital in Madison. She and my dad split when I was a kid, and she's been nursing ever since."

"Do you have a lot of brothers and sisters?"

He shook his head. "Just the one brother. He's living in Florida now."

"So, who spends holidays with her?"

"She goes to her mom's. This is our first year to be apart for the holidays, but I can't get away, and neither can she. We'll Skype, and it'll be fine."

Rikki realized then that he'd be spending the holiday alone too, and she hated that for him. "Well, whatever happens, we'll have to spend the holiday together. I'll be part of the Culpepper craziness, but I'm sure one more wouldn't hurt anything."

He dropped a kiss on her nose. "I think that sounds wonderful." He stood. "And on that note, it's time for me to head out. It's getting late, and I have a counseling session at eight."

She didn't ask when she'd see him again, but she wanted to. Why did her life seem so empty when he wasn't there? She was getting too involved already. "Sounds good. I'll see you at rehearsal on Friday night."

"I'll be by for lunch tomorrow. And maybe we can have dinner tomorrow night."

"That sounds nice."

"I loved your cooking by the way. Sorry I forgot to kiss your feet."

She laughed, heading toward the door. She watched him shrug into his coat, and then he walked toward her, pulling her to him. "Goodnight, my love. Sleep well."

She wrapped her arms around him and just held him for a moment. "You too."

6

The Christmas tree lighting in the town square was beautiful. Rikki was surprised how well she handled the crowd as long as she was close to Ben. She held his gloved hand the whole time, and she felt perfectly safe.

He left her once to get hot chocolate for both of them, and she found herself growing increasingly nervous until he came back to her and handed her the Styrofoam cup he'd purchased for her. "You were starting to panic, weren't you?"

She nodded. "As soon as you left, I started looking around me, trying to figure out which man would put me in his car and drive off. I'm like one of those soldiers with PTSD, and you're like the dog who calms me." She hid a smile behind her cup as she took a sip.

"I don't know how I feel about being compared to a therapy dog."

"At least I'm not comparing you to one of those dogs who runs around with a barrel of whisky tied to his neck!"

"A Saint Bernard? You cannot be comparing me to a Saint Bernard now! I feel so abused!"

"Oh, hush. I'll kiss you all better later!"

Ben grinned at her. "Don't say that too loud. It sounded a lot naughtier than I think you meant it."

Rikki felt the heat rising in her cheeks. She hadn't meant anything dirty by her words, but she could see where he'd gotten that. "Be nice. Let's go see what the vendors are selling."

They walked toward the row of vendors selling their Christmas wares. There were booths selling Christmas dolls, tree ornaments, wreaths, and dozens of other Christmas items. It was fun to walk through and see what was there.

By the time they'd walked the length of the row, Rikki had purchased several different things for her family and friends. She found the perfect ornament for Valerie—a pregnant woman. For her mother, she found an ornament proclaiming that she was a grandmother, and got the same thing for Linda. There were a lot of babies that would soon be coming into her world, and she loved it.

Finally, after spending several hours walking around the square, talking to the different people they both knew and shopping, Ben said, "I should get you home. We have a big day tomorrow."

"I'm probably going to miss service. Grace said she and Marcus would drive us to the airport."

"I can't miss, but if you three would pick me up at the church, I'll have my suitcase in my car. We'll take off as soon as the sermon is over."

"You can't miss? Ever?"

"Well, sometimes I can, but I'm giving my first sermon here tomorrow. Brother Anthony said that the church needs fresh blood, and it might as well be mine."

Rikki laughed. "That sounds like Brother Anthony." She

thought for a moment about the time. "I can come. It'll be tight, but if you can make it, then I can too."

"I'd like you to be there for my first sermon here."

"That's all you had to say. Of course, I'll be there."

On the drive back to the Culpepper Ranch, he peppered her with questions about her sister and Jesse. "They seem to be really in love. How long have they known each other?"

"They met when they auditioned for the show. This is their fifth season, so it's been close to five years? I think?"

"And it took them that long to marry? You said he was in love with her from day one."

"He was, and I think she was in love with him. She was dating Curtis, though, and he was controlling. He did everything he could to keep them apart."

It was the first time she'd said Curtis's name to him when she hadn't seemed to be overcome with fear. He'd take that as a win. "And you said she broke it off with him and married Jesse the same day?"

"Yeah, Jesse talked her into flying to Vegas with him to marry. Mom and I didn't even know 'til the next day." She shook her head. "It's amazing how perfect they are together. I'm glad they finally figured it out."

"When did they marry?"

"In March. She got pregnant almost immediately, which is great. I get to have a little nephew. They had to marry them in the show really quick to cover the pregnancy, but neither of them complained."

"And we're also going to meet others from the show?"

"Well, I'm not sure, but I think we'll see Amber and probably Bob. You've met Bob, though, right?"

"Bob Bodefeld? Yeah, I met him and May at church. I like May a lot."

"She's really awesome. Did you know she's a romance

writer?" Rikki asked. She'd been reading May's novels for a lot longer than she'd known the woman's real name.

"Really?"

"Yeah, but she uses a pen name, so you'd never know unless she told you. She lives less than a mile from the set. Hopefully we'll get to stay with them."

"You don't want to stay with your sister and Jesse?"

"They live in a trailer on the set. It would be strange."

"I can see that." He pulled into Linda's driveway and got out of the car, walking around to open her door. "So, I guess I'll see you at church tomorrow. With your suitcase."

"I'm glad you agreed to go with me. I'm excited to see Valerie." She was even more excited for Valerie and Jesse to get to know him, though. She couldn't wait.

He pressed a quick kiss to her lips and waiting until she went inside before turning back to his car. He planned to come home engaged to Rikki, no matter what it took.

Rikki sat toward the middle of the church for Ben's sermon the following morning. It was the first time she hadn't sat in the very back row, ready for a quick escape. It felt odd to be so close to the front, but the first time his eyes met hers during the service, she felt comfortable. There were people on either side of her, but she knew them, and that made it easier.

Little Corinne sat on her right side, and as soon as the sermon was over, she stood up and did a little spin. She was wearing her tutu and butterfly wings over her pants and blouse, which made Rikki smile. "How does she sleep in her butterfly wings?" she asked Patience.

Patience shook her head. "I've finally got her to where

she'll take them off to take a bath and to sleep. She even wears them to school."

"When you marry Pastor Benjamin, I'm going to spin down the aisle with the flowers, okay?" Corinne asked.

Rikki blinked a couple of times. "What?"

"When you ask me to be your flower girl, I'm going to spin instead of walking. I have my own flower girl style, and I've done it before, so you just need to smile and let me do my thing, okay? This will be my fourth wedding!"

"I—what?"

Patience patted Rikki's arm. "The whole town has been planning your wedding for almost a week. Get used to it. That's just how Culpepper is."

Rikki sighed. "That's great. My wedding is being planned without me." She got to her feet and nodded at Ben who was hurrying toward the back of the church. She'd ridden into church with Marcus and Grace, so her suitcase was already in the back of Marcus's truck.

She met up with Ben at the back of the church, smiling shyly. "Your sermon was wonderful. I was a little surprised by the topic, but I enjoyed it."

"Brother Anthony chose my topic. As a single pastor, I had no desire to preach on abstinence until marriage, but there was no choice. At all."

"You seemed a little uncomfortable with the topic, but it was still good."

"Yeah. Well, I made it work. Are you ready?"

She nodded. "Let's get out of here."

Grace walked over and linked her arm through Rikki's. "Marcus sent me in to get you two. We have to leave now unless you want to miss your flight."

"Marcus is being overdramatic," Rikki said. "We have

three hours before our flight. An hour to get to the airport and two hours to wait for our flight. We'll be fine."

Still, they hurried out to the truck and climbed in, buckling immediately. Rikki felt odd to be taking a trip with Ben, but she was excited as well. She couldn't wait until she could see just how round her sister had gotten. She and Valerie were both tiny women, and the last time she'd seen her she'd looked like she'd swallowed a basketball with two full months to go. She should look very interesting by now.

They got their boarding passes as soon as they got to the airport, and Rikki looked at hers and laughed. "Valerie got us first class. She knew I'd have flown coach."

Ben looked at his ticket. "I've never flown first. Have you?"

"Only when I was going somewhere with my sister. I thought she'd put us in coach if she wasn't with us."

Two hours later they were on the plane. He stretched out his legs with a smile. "I've never sat on an airplane that had enough room for my long legs."

She shrugged. "I fit pretty well into the coach seats, so I don't mind flying cheap."

The stewardess came to get their pre-flight drink orders, and Rikki pulled out her phone to text Valerie and let her know they were on their way. A woman who was walking by stopped and stared at Rikki for a moment. "You look almost exactly like that actress. Valerie Dobson."

"I'm her younger sister." Rikki thought for a moment about correcting the woman and telling her that her sister was Valerie Savoy now, but she didn't. What difference did it make?

"Oh, so you're the one who got kidnapped! That must have been rough."

Rikki simply smiled. "It wasn't a walk in the park."

"Well, you tell your sister that we're all praying for her to have a healthy baby."

"I will. Thank you for caring about her so much."

"Oh, *Lazy Love* is the best show on television. We all just love Valerie. I think we were all more excited for their wedding than they were."

Rikki turned to Ben as the woman walked away. "I hate when people recognize me as looking like Valerie. I love my sister, but being linked to a kidnapping is not the way I want to be known for the rest of my life."

"You could be known as a pastor's wife, if you'd prefer. I know how to arrange it."

"One of these days, you're going to say something like that, and I'm going to agree, and you're not going to know how to react."

He laughed. "Yes, I will. I'll break into song."

"What song?"

"*Hallelujah*."

She smiled, pulling the pillow from the back of the seat in front of her, where she'd tucked it as soon as she'd gotten onto the plane. "I'm not a good flyer, so I'm going to sleep the whole way. I hope you don't mind."

"Of course not. I brought my iPad, and I'm going to play with my puzzle app."

"Puzzle app?"

He held up the iPad. "I got a jigsaw puzzle app. I love puzzles, but they take up too much room, and they're a pain to tuck away. With the app, I can do a whole puzzle quickly, and even if I don't, it'll be there waiting for me later."

"Okay, you play puzzle, and I'll sleep." She put the pillow against his shoulder, and rested her head on it.

He smiled at her, wondering if she realized just how

comfortable she'd become with him in a very short time. If only she'd take his proposals seriously...

Jesse and Valerie were both waiting in baggage claim when they got to DFW airport. Rikki flew at her sister, hugging her tight. "I've missed you!" They'd grown a great deal closer since Valerie's marriage.

Valerie kissed Rikki's cheek before turning her attention to Ben. "It's good to see you again, Pastor Benjamin."

"Please just call me Ben. I don't want to be Pastor Benjamin to you. I want to be the man who's in love with your sister."

Rikki stared at him. "In love?"

"Why else would I keep trying to convince you to marry me?" Ben asked, shaking his head at her. He held his hand out to Jesse. "Good to see you again."

"You too. Are you guys hungry? We can stop somewhere on the way to Wiggieville if you want."

"That sounds good," Rikki said. "I think Ben ate on the plane, but I slept the whole time. His shoulder makes a good pillow."

"Jesse's does too. I always sleep on flights."

Rikki studied Valerie for a moment. "You're getting huge."

Valerie laughed, resting her hand on the top of her belly. "I feel very, very round. But I love being pregnant. I think we'll have a dozen kids."

When Jesse didn't respond, Valerie poked him. "Did you hear me? I said, 'I think we'll have a dozen kids.'"

Jesse looked at Ben, ignoring his wife. "So how did you two meet?"

Ben raised an eyebrow. He could tell Jesse was trying not to comment on the dozen kids thing. "The same way I met you guys. In church. She was hiding in the back row, so I sat next to her."

"I've never seen her this happy. I didn't meet her until after the incident."

"The incident?" Rikki asked. "My kidnapping is now 'the incident?' Did you tell him to call it that?" She wished everyone would just quit pussyfooting around the whole thing and call a spade a spade. Calling it a diamond did no good.

Valerie shook her head. "He came up with it all on his own. See? He's not just another pretty face!"

Rikki laughed. "And here I thought that head was totally empty!"

The luggage started coming out then, and the men paid close attention to the carousel. While they were watching, Rikki talked to Valerie. "Where are we going to stay?" She knew Valerie would have put anyone else up in the hotel in Wiggieville, but since that's where she'd been when Valerie had taken her place with Curtis, she wouldn't be there.

"You're going to stay with me, and Ben is going to stay with Bob and May. We thought he'd be more comfortable if you were staying in separate places. It wouldn't be good if it got back to the congregation that the two of you were staying together when you came here."

"Good point." Rikki sighed. "So, tell me what you think of him!"

"He's tall. Handsome. Seems to care about you a great deal. Are you going to marry him?"

Rikki shrugged. "I honestly don't know. I'm a little worried that I'm falling for him too fast, if that makes any sense. I'm comfortable with him, and he makes me calm in a crowd. Did you notice I haven't had a panic attack since we got here?"

Valerie grinned. "I didn't until you pointed it out. Good job!"

"I know. Something about having him close is very calming. Sometimes."

"Only sometimes?" Valerie asked with a frown.

"Well, sometimes he gets me all hot and bothered," Rikki whispered, blushing. She was embarrassed to talk about it, but if you couldn't talk about things like that with your pregnant sister, who could you talk about them with?

"Marry him."

"What? Just like that? You don't want to get to know him better?"

"I think you're like me. Only one man in my whole life has ever made me feel anything sexual, and I married him. He's obviously the man God made just for you."

Rikki frowned. "You think?"

"I do think so. Marry him. He'll make you happy."

Ben walked over with their luggage, looking back and forth between the two sisters. "What are you two talking about?"

"Sister stuff," Valerie responded before Rikki could start sputtering. "Let's stop and eat on the way back. I have a craving."

Rikki groaned. "Don't tell me. Tacos."

"Well, it is Sunday."

Jesse rolled his eyes. "She said the same thing yesterday, except Saturday. She's killing me."

"Well, at least Tex-Mex has other food. You could have a burrito. Or enchiladas. Or fajitas! Oh man, I need some Tex-Mex. Fajitas for this girl."

Valerie linked her arm with Rikki's and led her toward the exit to the building. "Tacos. I'm having tacos."

Ben looked over at Jesse. "Now I understand why Rikki was thrilled to have burgers and not tacos on our first date."

"Tacos used to be my favorite food," Jesse lamented. "Now I'm so sick of them I don't even want to hear the word."

"But the baby needs them!" Valerie protested.

"Tacos it is." Jesse looked at Ben and shook his head. "I hope you like them, because we'll have them every day while you're here."

"I love tacos. I'll be Valerie's taco buddy."

"Good. Someone has to be."

"May's a good taco buddy!" Valerie called over her shoulder.

"She works too much though. You only get tacos with her once or twice a week."

"Good point. Okay, you're my newly designated taco buddy," Valerie said to Ben. "I hope you plan to take your duties seriously."

"Of course. I'm a serious kind of man after all."

Rikki smiled to herself. Ben was getting along great with Valerie and Jesse. Maybe her sister was right, and she should marry him. Maybe.

7

The foursome stopped for dinner on the way to Wiggieville, and they all went to the set together. As soon as they arrived, Jesse called Bob and May to come over, so they could get to know Ben a little before he went home with them for the night.

When May walked in, Rikki hurried toward her and hugged her tight. "It's good to see you!"

May smiled. "There's so much of me to see right now." She patted her belly affectionately.

"I hope you two are taking belly to belly pictures every month for a scrapbook."

May laughed, looking at Valerie. "We haven't really discussed the possibility, but I guess we could."

"Well, you need to do more than just eat tacos together."

"I second that!" Bob said, waving at Rikki. He knew not to get too close. All the men she knew did.

Rikki swallowed hard and walked over to Bob, hugging him. "It's good to see you, Bob."

Bob looked at her with surprise. "You look happy. I'm glad." He patted her back awkwardly.

Ben walked over and slid his arm around Rikki's waist, holding his hand out to Bob. "I'm Ben. I'm the associate pastor of the church in Culpepper."

"We met the last time May and I were in town. We're not there every three weeks yet like Valerie and Jesse, but we'll get there. We're doing some renovations on the house we bought right now. Hopefully we'll be able to start living there part time after Bobette is born." Bob shrugged. "I think it's going to be a good place for us to live. A small town with a real community like we portray in *Lazy Love*."

"It's a good place to live. Very community focused, and the women are gorgeous." Ben was looking at Rikki as he said the last of it.

Bob laughed. "I can't argue with that." He looked over at Jesse. "Why don't we show him the set? We can chat while we walk."

Jesse nodded. "We'll leave the girls alone for a few minutes. Have you ever been on a television set?"

Ben shook his head, intrigued. He was very interested to hear what the men wanted to talk to him about. "Would you mind?" he asked Rikki.

She shook her head. "Absolutely not. We came here for you to get to know everyone better."

"All right. I'll be back soon."

As soon as they were gone, Rikki turned to May. "Well? What do you think of him?"

May shrugged. "He's no Bob... What really matters is what you think of him."

Rikki took a deep breath, admitting aloud what she'd realized days before. "I think I'm in love with him."

Valerie clapped her hands, turning from where she was digging in the fridge. "I knew it!"

"Valerie, you sit and talk to May. You're too pregnant to be bending like that. What are you looking for?"

"There's some taco meat in a Tupperware bowl from last night. Would you heat up the meat, and make some nachos? I'm starving!"

Rikki blinked at her sister a few times. "Are you kidding? We just ate!"

"Baby Amber's hungry."

May giggled. "So is Bobbette. I think it's been at least an hour since she's been fed."

Rikki just shrugged, finding the taco meat. "Do you want me to spread the meat over chips, add cheese, and bake it all in the oven?"

"Sounds good!" Valerie said encouragingly. "Now, tell us more about Ben. Is he a native of Culpepper?"

Rikki talked while she worked. "No, he hasn't been there as long as I have. He's very kind. He's taken over the church's Christmas pageant, and he's finding spots for all the kids, even the ones who have less than a thimble-full of talent. He's even creating a part for this little girl who can dance. Oh, you know Patience, Valerie. It's for her step-daughter, Corinne!"

"Oh, I think I've met Corinne. Isn't she the one who runs around in a tutu and butterfly wings all the time?"

May grinned. "I've got to meet this kid!"

Rikki laughed. "You really do. She's awesome! Anyway, she came up to me at church today and told me when I'm ready for her services she'll be spinning down the aisle."

"Her services?" Valerie asked.

"She's some sort of professional flower girl. Probably only in her own mind, but she told me she's done four weddings, and she'd be happy to do ours. As long as we let her spin." Rikki shook her head. "What do you even say to that?"

"You're not engaged, are you?" May asked, before looking at Valerie. "You never tell me anything! I thought she was bringing the man she was dating here, and he's her fiancé?"

Rikki giggled, and Valerie looked over at her. "You have no idea how good it is to hear you laughing again. I was so worried about you."

Rikki slid the cookie sheet full of nachos into the oven before sitting at the table with her sister and May. "I feel like I've just woken up from a deep sleep. I've been walking around in a fog for months, not letting myself feel anything, because I was worried I'd feel too much pain. It's like I was Sleeping Beauty and it took Ben's kiss to wake me. How corny is that?"

May shrugged. "I'm a romance writer. I love corny!"

"We're not engaged. He's hinted that he wants to marry me, but we've only been dating a week."

"A whole week? Bob and I married six days after we met. What's the hold up?"

"Maybe I'm not as crazy as you?" Rikki made a face.

Valerie laughed. "That's my sister, coming back! I see the girl who yelled at me for being famous and ruining her life rearing her beautiful head."

Rikki sighed. "I'm sorry I did that. I was such a brat."

"You weren't. You just got tired of living in my shadow, and honestly, who could blame you? I love what I do, but I never really thought about how it would be for my almost identical kid sister."

"You didn't do anything wrong, Valerie. I was just a kid who thought her life was falling apart, because her sister was famous. It was really stupid." Rikki shook her head.

"And it's my own fault I was kidnapped. I thought if I went with Curtis, I could get him to help me break you and Jesse up, and then Jesse would be free for me. You two were made to be together, and I was a stupid kid throwing a tantrum."

Valerie covered Rikki's hand with hers. "Oh no. You haven't been living with that guilt, have you? I promise you Curtis would have gotten you into that van either way. He was determined to do whatever he could to get me back, and he knew that I'd never let anything happen to you."

Rikki swiped at a tear. "I think I do know that, which makes it so much worse. I shouldn't have thought about breaking you up. I—I don't know that I'd have been able to do the same thing in your place. You're the strong sister. The good sister. What on earth am I doing dating a pastor?"

Valerie grinned. "You're dating a pastor because you're a good person. You'll make a great pastor's wife. Think about it for a minute...could someone who had never been through hardship be able to truly empathize with a person in pain? I think you'll be great in that role if that's what you choose."

"Do you really?"

May looked between the sisters, leaning forward. "I probably shouldn't have been here for this whole thing, but I have to agree with Valerie. Rikki, you're an amazing young woman. You're strong and beautiful. You should do whatever is right for you, and let go of the guilt you feel for your own kidnapping. After all, you're the only one who was hurt."

"I put my sister in the role of having to risk her life for me. How can I forgive myself for that?"

Valerie leaned forward and kissed her sister's cheek. "You can do it, because I don't think you did anything wrong. I understand. So, you have to forgive yourself, because truly, there's nothing to forgive."

The timer on the stove buzzed, and Rikki jumped up to get the nachos, thinking about what Valerie had said. If she told the truth then…well, maybe she was good enough to marry Ben after all. If he mentioned it again, she'd think about it. How could she not? He was a good man, and she loved him. She really did!

When the men came back into the trailer, they saw what the women were eating, and Bob groaned. "May, if Bobbette is born with cheese for hair, I'm blaming no one but you!"

"She needs tacos! How many times do I have to tell you that?" May glared at her husband, making Rikki giggle.

Ben walked around to stand behind Rikki, one hand going to her shoulder possessively. The walk with the men had been very enlightening. He'd had no idea how protective her new brother-in-law and his best friend felt about her. They'd given him the 'be careful' speech, but then they'd also gone on to give advice about how to get her to marry him. He'd try it. He'd try anything at this point. In Culpepper time, they should have been married days ago! "You're not having nachos?"

Rikki shook her head adamantly. "I'm not even hungry. Valerie swore up and down little Amber would starve to death if she didn't feed him, so I made nachos for her and May."

Bob groaned. "You're not really calling that boy Amber!"

Jesse shook his head. "No, we're not. Valerie calls him that just to annoy me, I think."

"Why would I do something just to annoy you?" Valerie asked with an innocent look on her face.

"Because that's what you do. Why I thought I needed to marry you is beyond me…"

"Because you can't imagine life without me." Valerie's voice was soft, but powerful. No one in the room had any doubt that she spoke the truth.

Rikki looked over her shoulder at Ben, and that's when she realized that Jesse's truth was also hers. She couldn't imagine living the rest of her life without the man standing behind her. The next time he mentioned marriage to her, she was going to jump at the chance. How could she not when she loved him as much as she did? He was her oasis in the desert. Her port in a storm. Her—she almost groaned aloud at her constant maudlin thoughts. He was hers. What else mattered?

Bob walked over behind May, resting his hands on both of her shoulders. "When you two are done feeding the babies, we should get home. I know a certain writer who needs to get her word count in tonight, even if we do have guests."

May shrugged. "I actually got most of it in today. I only have another thousand words to go, and that's twenty minutes work."

"Good. You and Bobbette need rest."

Ben frowned at Bob. "Are you really naming that poor child Bobbette?"

Bob shrugged. "I think it has a nice ring to it. You don't like it?"

"No, I really don't."

May smiled. "We'll call her Bobbi. I think the world should be entirely peopled with Bobs."

"Sounds good to me! And I'll be King Bob!"

"Court Jester Bob. Quit trying to elevate yourself to king status." May ate her last nacho and pushed away from the table. She looked over at Ben. "Are you ready?"

Ben looked down at Rikki. He was ready all except for

kissing his girl goodnight, but that would be strange in front of all these people. Rikki seemed to know what he was thinking, because she stood and raised her lips for his kiss. He pressed a light kiss to her mouth before walking toward the door. "I'm ready."

Just as his hand was about to reach the doorknob, Rikki called out, "Hey, Ben?"

"Yeah?"

"Dream of me."

Ben smiled, thinking of what he'd told her after their first kiss. "How could I dream of anything else?"

———

RIKKI WOKE EARLY the following morning, even earlier than usual. She rolled out of bed and went to the bathroom to shower, before going into the kitchen. Jesse and Valerie weren't out yet, so she decided to make breakfast. After digging through the fridge, she found the makings for breakfast tacos—she knew it wasn't exactly what Valerie was craving, but the effort would make her happy.

When Valerie came out a short while later, hiding a yawn behind her hand, she smiled. "What are you doing up so early? You're never up early."

"I don't know. I woke up and realized I was in Texas with my sister, and didn't want to waste a single minute of my time here."

Valerie smiled. "Something smells good. What are you making?"

Rikki carefully rolled up some of the eggs, sausage, and cheese mixture; put it on a plate, and handed it to her sister. "Breakfast tacos. I know they're not exactly what you're craving, but I figured they'd make you happy."

"Of course, they do." Valerie walked to the table and took a huge bite, chewing slowly. "Did you make any decisions?"

Rikki nodded. "If he asks again, I'm going to say yes. I think I'm ready. Now that I know you forgive me for being stupid." She rolled up several tacos, putting one on a plate, and leaving the others. Walking to the table, she sat down and took a bite. "Hey, these aren't bad."

"Not at all." Valerie watched her sister for a moment. "I was worried I'd never see you smile again. I think marrying Ben will be the most brilliant thing you've ever done. Especially since you said he makes your heart beat faster."

Rikki smiled at her sister's delicate phrasing. "I'm definitely warm for his form."

Valerie laughed. "Maybe you can have half of those dozen kids I keep warning Jesse about."

"Half? Six would be an awful lot, don't you think? Maybe May can have three, and Amber can have three. Then each of us only need to have three, but there will still be a dozen kids running around."

"That's not a bad idea! I don't think Amber's in any hurry, though. Do you want to see her today? I told her you'd be here this week, and she said she could come by today while Nicki is in school and John is working."

"I'd love that! I want to ride a little too, if that's okay."

Valerie nodded. "I'm sure that's fine. The horses are available for us to use when we're not filming. Bob rides quite a bit."

"I don't know if Ben rides or not, but if not, he can learn. Would you mind hooking up with Amber for lunch? And Ben and I can ride this afternoon?"

"Works for me. I never thought of you as someone who

would love riding, but I remember how cathartic it was for you after the kidnapping." Valerie got up and got herself another taco. "These really are good. I need to make them more."

"There have to be fast food places that sell them around here."

"I think Whataburger does, but there isn't one in Wiggieville. I'd have to go to Weatherford, and it's easier to just make it myself than drive that far."

Rikki shook her head. "As long as you have your priorities straight."

Jesse wandered out of the bedroom then, looking at the sisters for a minute before glaring at Rikki. "You made her breakfast tacos! What is wrong with you?"

Rikki shrugged. "I figured it would make her happy, and I was right. Don't you want a happy wife?"

"Sure, I do, but I want less tacos in my world too!" He took three and piled them on a plate, walking to the table. "But as long as they're here, I shouldn't let them go to waste."

Valerie shook her head. "You gripe about them even as you're eating them. You should be thanking Rikki for the culinary delight she made for us."

"Next time I come down I'll make kolaches. Patience will teach me soon. She keeps promising."

"If you marry Ben, I don't think you'll get to visit real often," Valerie said with a frown.

Jesse looked between the sisters. "Wait, you're thinking of actually marrying him? He told me you'd talked about it, but I thought it was all in his head. I had no idea you were really considering it!"

Rikki shrugged. "I love him. He makes me happy. I think I realized last night that it was time to say yes, when Valerie said that you couldn't imagine life without her. That's how I feel about Ben."

He studied her for a minute, before nodding. "I can't imagine a better reason to marry. I have a feeling he'll be asking again soon."

"Do you know something I don't?"

"If I told you what I know, I'd be breaking the man code. Don't you know there are rules?"

Rikki sighed. "I think I'll do the dishes then. It's got to be better than listening to man code explanations."

8

Rikki and Valerie spent the morning together, talking about the baby and everything else life had thrown at them. "Do you ever resent Dad for taking off?" Rikki asked.

Valerie shrugged. "He contacted me over the summer. He said he had been following my career. I decided not to see him."

"Did he ask about me?" Rikki felt childish for asking, but she'd always missed growing up with a father. At least Valerie had seven years with him. She'd only had one.

"He asked how you were doing after the kidnapping. He'd read about it online. I didn't really answer, but I offered your phone number. I'm guessing he never called."

Rikki shook her head, determined not to care. Enough had gone on since their father had left that his abandonment was the least of her worries. "I wonder where the guys are today."

"I'm not sure," Valerie said, obviously happy with the change of topic. "Jesse said something about doing an errand with Ben. He's going to pick up tacos and burgers on his way back from town, and they'll get here around noon. Amber is supposed to be here at eleven."

"It'll be good to see her. I always feel like she's my sister too."

"She feels a connection to you as well." Valerie stood and wandered into the nursery. "I haven't shown you the baby's room yet!"

The sisters spent the rest of the morning puttering around the baby's room. Valerie showed Rikki the things fans had sent them. "We have enough handmade clothes for six babies," she said with a laugh.

"What are you really naming the baby?" Rikki asked. "I know you don't want it to get out, but it's not like I'm going to announce it on Twitter. And I *am* your favorite sister. Well, your favorite real sister. Amber's probably your favorite…"

Valerie rolled her eyes. "We're naming him Jaron. Jaron Samuel Savoy."

"I like it! It's unusual, but not so far out there no one will be able to pronounce it."

There was a knock at the door and then a voice called out, "Honey, I'm home!"

Rikki rushed from the nursery into Amber's waiting arms. "It's so good to see you!"

Amber held Rikki at arm's length for a moment. She hadn't seen her since the week following the kidnapping, and she seemed to be assessing her. "You've lost some weight, but you look happy. I've been worried about you."

"I am happy. I still have nightmares. I still freak out over stupid things, but deep down, I think I'm happy. Wait 'til you meet him."

Amber took Rikki's hand and pulled her to the couch. "Tell me everything about him!"

When the men walked in the door forty-five minutes later, Amber looked at Ben. "You'd better be who she thinks you are."

"Excuse me?" Ben looked surprised at the vehemence behind the words.

"You'd better not hurt my friend."

Ben looked back and forth between Amber and Rikki. "And you are?"

"Amber Knight. I play Valerie's sister on *Lazy Love*, so as Rikki has pointed out more than once, we're practically sisters. Don't hurt her."

"I wouldn't. I love her." He said the words so simply that Rikki's heart skipped a beat.

She stood and walked to him, wrapping her arms around his waist. "I missed you this morning."

He held her close. "We had an errand."

"How can you have an errand when you live in another state?"

"We brought lunch," he said, effectively changing the subject. "Tacos for Valerie and me and burgers for the rest of you."

Rikki frowned at him. "You're not going to tell me where you went?"

Jesse stepped in then. "Did Valerie show you the baby's room? It looks to me like Mickey Mouse vomited in there."

Rikki looked back and forth between the two men, but she didn't push it. "I saw it. I like all the Mickey stuff. That baby is going to feel right at home when his Auntie Rikki takes him to Disney World."

"His Auntie Rikki isn't taking baby Amber anywhere without his Auntie Amber," Amber said.

Jesse groaned. "You all need to stop referring to my unborn son as Amber. You're making me crazy!"

Amber wrinkled her nose. "I think Amber is a perfect name for a boy or a girl. And if you don't name this one Amber, I'll just hound you until you name the next one Amber. Amber is the name to remember. Amber. Amber. Amber." She said the words in a hypnotic voice, as if trying to force Jesse to agree to naming the baby what she wanted.

"Oh please! We're not naming him Amber. Get a grip." He set the bag of food on the table and watched as his wife riffled through it, obviously desperate to get to her tacos.

Amber looked at Jesse. "How long has it been since you fed that poor baby tacos?"

"She had them for dinner last night. Then she somehow conned Rikki into making her and May nachos. And Rikki made breakfast tacos this morning. My wife and baby are *not* starving for tacos!"

They all sat down and dug into the fast food. "I'm going to have to work out for an extra hour thanks to this burger," Amber lamented. "But man, it tastes *good*!"

After lunch, Rikki stood up. "I want to go riding. Will you come with me, Ben?"

Ben nodded. "I'd love to."

"Have you ridden much?"

He shook his head. "No, but I've ridden some. Mostly at camp where the horses plod along on their trails without much coaxing, but I can figure out what to do if I have to."

Jesse stood up. "I'll go with you so they'll let you take the horses." He led them in the direction of the stable. "Valerie's and my horses haven't been ridden as much this season, because of her pregnancy. If you wouldn't mind taking them out, they could use the exercise."

"I love Valerie's horse on the show. Her name is Buttercup, right?"

"On the show, it is. In real life, it's Autumn."

"Oh, I like that. I'm riding Autumn then."

Ben looked at Jesse. "Is your horse gentle enough for a novice?"

"Definitely. I couldn't ride when I got the part. I spent every spare minute with Trevor, and together we figured it out."

"Your horse's name is Trevor? Okay, I'll take Trevor then."

When they got to the stable, the man in charge offered to saddle the horses, and Ben didn't argue. "We'll be back in an hour or two," he told Jesse.

"Be careful. If you break my sister-in-law, I'll have to deal with my wife. No one wants to deal with my wife."

Ten minutes later, they were riding side by side toward the open meadow that separated the set from May's house. Once they reached the meadow, Ben pulled back on the reins and swung his right leg over the back of the horse, waiting as Rikki did the same.

"You're a better rider than you let on!" she told him.

He shrugged. "Maybe I worked at the camp and taught others how to ride. Something like that."

She shook her head, stepping toward him. "I feel like we're constantly being watched here. I need less other people and more kissing."

He grinned. "I was thinking the same thing myself a little while ago. This ride was a brilliant idea."

"I thought so. Of course, it was mine, so I would think it was brilliant."

He caught her by the waist and pulled her to him, his mouth descending for a more passionate kiss than they'd shared before. "I want to ask you something."

Her breath caught in her throat. *Is he going to propose again?* She knew just what she'd say if he did! "What's that?"

He dropped to one knee, right there in the wet Texas grass. "Rikki Dobson, will you do me the honor of being my wife?" He held out a ring box to her, and opened it, so she could see the ring he'd chosen.

Rikki took the ring and slipped it on her finger, nodding emphatically. "I thought you'd never ask!"

"I've asked and asked!" he protested.

"Well, I thought you'd never ask properly. You know, on one knee in a field somewhere in Texas."

"Why did it need to be in a field somewhere in Texas?"

Rikki shrugged. "I don't know, but this seems like the perfect setting, doesn't it? When do you want to get married?"

"Wednesday?" he asked. He knew he was pushing it, but he didn't want to wait. They'd be getting married in Culpepper after all, and Culpepper couples didn't have long engagements. Not even a week long usually.

She bit her lip for a moment, thinking about the logistics of putting a small wedding together before Wednesday. "Okay."

"Really?" He couldn't believe he'd gotten her to agree to marry him so quickly, but he wasn't going to argue. He got to his feet, pulled her into his arms, and twirled her around. "I can't believe you agreed."

She smiled up at him, feeling as if the whole universe had opened up to give her everything she wanted. "I love you. How could I keep putting it off?"

Ben looked down into her eyes. "You really love me?"

She nodded, her eyes twinkling. "Of course, I do. I don't marry just any guy on a moment's notice!"

He kissed her again, his hands pulling her close. "I can't wait to have you as my wife."

Rikki sighed. "Me neither. No more saying goodnight at the door. We can hold each other all night long."

"It sounds heavenly." He kissed her once more. "Should we go back and tell the others?"

Rikki shook her head. "Not yet. Let's glory in it for another minute or two, and I'm going to call the bakery and get them started on a cake."

The phone calls were fast and easy, and twenty minutes later they were headed back to the set. They returned the horses and walked hand in hand back to Jesse and Valerie's trailer.

When they opened the door, they found her sister and husband sitting on the couch side by side. Jesse's hand was on Valerie's belly. "He's kicking," Valerie explained with a grin. "Everyone in the world has felt him kick except for Jesse. As soon as Jesse gets close he stops moving."

Jesse sighed. "And he did it again. Someday that baby is going to let me feel him move!"

"Probably after he's born," Valerie said with a smile.

"Can I feel him?" Rikki asked, fascinated by the baby's growth. She loved the idea of having a baby with Ben.

Valerie nodded. "Sure. I'll show you where to put your hand."

As soon as Rikki was close, Valerie took her hand and placed it on the side of her belly. "Right there."

Rikki smiled. "I can feel him! He's strong. Does it hurt?"

Valerie shook her head. "No, it feels strange, but it doesn't hurt at all." She looked down at the hand on her belly and squealed. "I see an engagement ring! You're getting married!" She pulled Rikki down awkwardly for a hug, until Rikki was mostly lying across her.

"I'm going to squish you and Amber!" Rikki protested. "Let me up."

Valerie let go of her sister, but quickly got to her feet, hugging her again. Then she turned and hugged Ben, whispering to him, "Take good care of her when I'm not there to do it."

"Always. Whether you're there or not," he whispered back.

She smiled. "I knew there was a reason I liked you!"

Jesse stepped forward and shook Ben's hand. "I told you that was the right size ring. Our ladies are the same size. Welcome to the family."

Ben smiled at Jesse's words. "Thank you. I'd say I got the pick of the litter, but I think we both got pretty special women."

"Oh, we definitely did."

When Rikki and Ben walked into baggage claim back in Wyoming the following day, Grace squealed, running to hug Rikki. "Another wedding! I have the cake done, and Corinne said to tell you she's been practicing her leaps for your wedding."

Rikki looked at Ben. "We have a flower girl all ready to go."

Ben grinned at that. "Brother Anthony said that we're turning into a ridiculously clichéd town, and we need to stop this wedding madness, but that he'd be ready to marry us at seven tomorrow evening."

Grace giggled. "That sounds just like Brother Anthony. At least he's going to remember your name."

"I'm not sure he even knows mine," Rikki said. "Maybe I should have it printed on my forehead for him."

Grace shook her head. "Do you have a dress yet? Do you want to wear mine?"

Rikki shrugged. "I have a nice white suit that I thought would work well. I'm going to wear that." She wished Valerie could be there, but there was no way she could travel.

"Have you told Linda yet?" Grace asked, pointing as the luggage started to come around the carousel. She obviously knew Ben would handle it, because she stayed where she was.

"Yeah, I called her. She cried. I don't know if it was because she was so happy I'm getting married or relieved that she's finally getting rid of her houseguest."

Grace laughed, watching as Ben hauled the luggage off the belt. "Sorry Marcus couldn't come. He had a deposition." She turned and led the way to her SUV.

Rikki looked at Ben. "Have you emailed the parents to let them know there won't be a rehearsal tomorrow after all?"

Ben nodded. "I did. I'm not leaving that to chance. Mrs. Pfaffenbach is concerned I'm taking my Christmas pageant duties too lightly, and that her Timmy might need a more experienced, dedicated director to bring out his true talent."

Rikki giggled. Timmy Pfaffenbach was the worst actor of all the children, and he couldn't carry a tune in a bucket. He had been given the job of the third wise man, who had no lines at all. "Well, you know Mrs. Pfaffenbach is always right about Timmy."

"Are you taking tomorrow off work too, Rikki?" Grace asked as they got into the vehicle.

Rikki shook her head. "No, I'm not planning on it. If I could get off an hour or two early, that would help though."

"Are you getting married in the church? Or at Linda's?" Grace asked.

Rikki had no idea. "I let Ben handle that."

Ben grinned. "I was happy to have something to do while they discussed all the other details of the wedding. We're getting married at Linda's. It's smaller and will be more private, and I think Rikki will feel more comfortable there."

"I will. Thank you." Rikki was constantly surprised at how thoughtful Ben was about her fears. She hadn't had a panic attack in over a week, and that was a record. She wanted to shout it from the rooftops, but she knew that no one would understand.

"Okay, so we're looking at how many guests?" Grace asked.

Ben answered for them. "I was thinking about twenty. Will that be enough people to watch Corinne dance down the aisle?"

"Oh, sure," Grace said. "An audience of one or five thousand. That girl has the right attitude about it all. She's going to perform for whoever is willing to watch her."

Rikki grinned. The girl had danced around the bakery enough that she knew Grace was telling the truth. "What else do we need to do to get ready?"

Grace shrugged. "I think you're set. You've got the pastor, a flower girl, and a preacher. What more do you need?"

"A matron of honor might be nice. Would you be willing?" Rikki asked.

"I'd love to! I still have the dress I wore for my twin's wedding, so I'll wear that."

"Sounds good to me." Rikki didn't care what anyone wore as long as they were decently covered.

"Are you going to live in town? Or at the ranch?" Grace asked.

"We haven't really talked about it," Rikki said with a frown. She turned to Ben who was in the backseat. "I have a two-bedroom apartment over Jesse and Valerie's garage. It's more than big enough for both of us. Do you want to live there? Or your place?"

"My place is no bigger than a postage stamp. It sounds like your place is the winner."

Rikki smiled. "I love my little apartment, but I've been afraid to live there without Jesse and Valerie. I won't be afraid if you're around." She was so thrilled that her fears were getting easier. She didn't know what she'd do without him. He was becoming her rock.

"Sounds good. I don't have a ton of stuff, but I'll pack up what I do have and get it moved over after the wedding." He loved saying the word wedding. When he used it, he thought of Rikki, and it felt like his heart was full. In just over twenty-four hours, she was going to be his wife, and he couldn't wait.

"Thanks for handling the wedding cake so fast," Rikki said.

Grace laughed. "You know I keep one mostly decorated in the freezer. I just had to add little pink roses, and I was done."

"Why pink?" Rikki asked.

"I'm not sure. I look at you and I think pink." She turned onto the highway that would take them into Culpepper. "Did you remember to hug Valerie for me?"

"I wouldn't forget. I even hugged Buttercup for you."

"She let you see Buttercup? Really?" Grace's voice was full of envy.

Rikki laughed, knowing that Grace was a huge fan of the

show. It was how she'd gotten the job at the bakery. "I even got to ride her."

"Okay, walk me through everything. Do you have pictures of yourself on the set?"

Rikki nodded. "I'll show you when we get to Linda's."

"You're the best!"

9

Rikki was in her room at Linda's house the following day, trying to get her breathing under control when Corinne danced her way into the room. "I'm wearing my favorite flower girl dress!" Corinne announced. "The pink one used to be my favorite, but it got too small, and then it didn't look good with my butterfly wings, so I had to get this one. It's lavender. Do you like lavender?"

Rikki smiled, thrilled for the diversion. "I love lavender. You look beautiful, Corinne. I'm glad you found a dress that looks so good with your wings."

Corinne did a little spin. "That's how I go down the aisle. It's the only way I do it, so don't worry when I start spinning."

Patience popped her head into the room, looking Rikki over. "Do you need help getting ready?"

Rikki shook her head. "I don't think so. How do I look?" She stood up from the foot of the bed where she'd been sitting. She was wearing a white suit she'd found one day while shopping that she'd thought she might wear to church, but she'd realized how impractical white was and wondered why she'd ever purchased it.

Patience studied her carefully. "I think you need just a little more lipstick, because we all know Pastor Benjamin is going to smudge it."

"Cuz he's going to kiss her, isn't he, Mama?"

"Yes, he is. It's part of the wedding ceremony."

Rikki hurried to the mirror and put her lipstick on. "Is he already out there?"

"Yes, he's pacing back and forth. I think he's worried that you're going to get scared and run."

Rikki laughed. "The thought had occurred to me."

"If you ask me, and I know you didn't, you should run toward that man. You've been happier since you started dating him than I've ever seen you. He's really good for you.

"He is good for me." Rikki took a deep breath. "I'm being silly. I'm in love with him, and he's just what I need in every way."

"Do you want me to go out and tell Brother Anthony it's time?"

"Don't we need to wait until everyone gets here?" Rikki asked, confused.

"Everyone's been here. We were supposed to get started fifteen minutes ago."

Rikki looked at the clock in surprise. "I've been sitting back here ready for an hour just staring at the wall."

"I should have checked on you sooner. I'm sorry!"

"No, I should have come out." Rikki sighed. "I'm not so good at this getting married thing."

"Nonsense. Brides are supposed to be late."

"Just not so late they freak their groom out, right?"

"No one knew if we should come check on you, so we waited. That was our mistake. Corinne finally said it was her job as your flower girl." Patience shrugged. "Grace probably should have done it as the matron of honor."

"I'm surprised Felicity didn't do it. She's pushier than the rest of you."

Patience laughed. "She's not pushy. She's just...special."

"Mama!" Corinne tugged on Patience's dress.

Patience looked down at Corinne. "Yes?"

"People are waiting to see me dance down the aisle with my flowers!"

"They sure are. I'll start the music." Patience hurried from the room, pulling Corinne along with her.

Rikki took a deep breath and stepped out into the hall. She would be the center of attention, which was hard, but she'd be married to Ben when it was done, and that was so worth it.

She heard music start, and then there was soft laughter. Grace hurried toward her. "I'm sorry! I didn't know you were ready! I should have checked on you."

Rikki grabbed Grace in a hug, kissing her cheek. "Thank you for being here for me. I should have let you know when I was ready."

"We're good?"

"Of course, we're good!" Rikki gave her friend a nudge. "And you're up!"

Grace grinned and walked down the hall to the living room where the wedding was taking place. Rikki watched her go and waited a minute before following.

As she walked, she felt the panic rise up within her, and after she turned the corner to walk into the living room, it became almost overwhelming. And then she saw Ben standing in front of Brother Anthony, his eyes filled with love. She walked to him and stood beside him, not looking at anyone else. If she could just concentrate on him, she could get through it.

Brother Anthony gave a small cough to clear his throat before beginning. "Dearly beloved, we are gathered here today to join this man and this woman in holy matrimony. Now I know we're all happy for them that they've decided to tie the knot and all, but I have to make it clear how I feel about all these fast weddings in Culpepper. There's only been one 'long engagement' since those Quinlan women showed up in town and turned it on its ear. And that engagement was barely enough time to let the ink dry on the marriage license! I ask you, what is in the water that two people can't give a pastor enough time to think about what he's going to say at a wedding after they get engaged? There is something wrong with this town, and it's a mighty wrong! We must fix this trend and return to a normal place, where people can wait three days after they get engaged to get married!"

Rikki looked at the amused look on Ben's face and did her best not to giggle. Brides weren't supposed to giggle in the middle of their wedding ceremonies, were they?

Brother Anthony looked out at the small crowd of people gathered there for the wedding. "Now, Lovie. I know what you're going to say. This isn't the time or place, but you always tell me it isn't the time or place! You never give me my soapbox to stand on, but this time, I'm just taking it! You hear me?"

"I hear ya, Tony! I guess this is as good a time as any since it's your assistant pastor up there getting married, and he can't very well run away from you!"

"All right then, now that I've said my piece, let's get you two hitched. Ben, do you promise to love, honor, and cherish your bride? 'Til death do you part? In sickness and health and all the other stuff you go through when you're married?"

Ben looked down into Rikki's eyes, stroking her cheek with one hand. "I do."

"And do you—the young lady with a man's name—do you take this man to be your husband? Love, honoring, and respecting him through sickness and health, rich and poor forever and ever amen?"

Rikki nodded before she answered. "I do. I really, really do!"

"Then I now pronounce you man and wife. Go ahead and kiss her so we can all watch and stuff."

Ben pulled her to him by the hand he held, lowering his head to kiss her softly. "I was afraid you'd run."

"I am kind of a flight risk, but I can't imagine not marrying you, so where would I go?"

He hugged her tightly, and then they turned to face everyone. He felt Rikki shudder beside him, and he slipped his arm around her waist. "I'm here, and you're going to be fine," he whispered softly.

"I am. I really am."

Felicity, who had been Facetiming the whole thing with Valerie, wiped away a tear. "They're married!" she squealed.

Rikki looked at Ben, still needing to keep her eyes on him and not on the people watching her. "I think people are happy for us."

"I know I am," he said with a grin.

Linda stood up then. "Okay, we're going to have some cake, and then we're going to kick these newlyweds out of my house. I think Rikki needs to be able to get out of here before we all make her as crazy as we are!"

Ben led Rikki over to the cake, which was on the

counter, separating the kitchen from the dining area. "We can cut the cake and go."

"Perfect," she whispered. "I have all my stuff packed."

Together they cut the cake and fed each other a bite. Brother Anthony stood watching them. "Good job getting it into each other's mouths. That whole smearing the cake all over each other's faces is just plain silly."

Ben nodded. "It is silly. And now we're running away from here."

"What's your hurry? Stay a while." Brother Anthony smiled, his eyes dancing with laughter. "I needed to talk to you about Sunday's sermon anyway."

Ben groaned inwardly. "Tomorrow. I'm getting my bride out of here." He knew Rikki wouldn't do well if asked to stay there much longer. Too many people were watching them, and it wasn't good for her at all. He took her hand and led her toward the hallway, knowing her things would be there. "Let's go!"

She smiled. "Are we leaving in one car or both?"

He groaned. "Hadn't thought about that. Why don't we take your car, and you can drop me off here on your way to work in the morning. I'm assuming you need to work."

"Yeah, I do. I've taken too much time off this week already."

She opened the door to her room, and he grabbed two suitcases. "Does this have everything you need for tonight? We can get the rest of your stuff when no one is around."

She grabbed a shoulder bag. "That's the bag I need. Let's take all three."

He nodded, not caring how much she wanted to take as long as she had what she needed. "We're heading to your apartment at Valerie's?"

"Yes, please. Did you pack clothes?"

"Of course, I did. I didn't want to have to run home after the wedding to get them." He let her precede him out of the room, and stopped almost immediately as she hugged Linda, who was waiting for them.

"Thank you for letting me stay here, and being my surrogate mom for a while. I don't know what I would have done without you."

"You're stronger than you think you are. You'd have done fine without me." Linda swiped a tear from her eye. "I'm proud of you. You've grown so much, and Ben is the right man for you. Be happy."

Rikki sniffled as she wiped her own tear away. "It's not like I won't be around anymore! I'll still come see you."

"But it won't be the same, and you know it. It hasn't been the same since you started seeing Ben. You've been busier and more involved with life. And that's so very good for you." With one last hug, Linda smiled. "Now go and be happy."

"I will." Rikki looked over Linda's shoulder to see Roy standing there listening. She walked to the older man and hugged him. "Your turn next!"

Roy grinned. "We'll see."

Rikki hurried toward the door, hoping no one else would try to stop them. She appreciated that everyone had come to her wedding, but she couldn't deal with that many people, so she needed to get out and soon.

She rushed out to the car, feeling the cold wind biting against her skin. *Why didn't I bring a coat? I have everything in the world but a coat! Too late. I'm not going back into that house with all those people for all the tea in China.*

She got into the car and started it, turning the heat on high and feeling the cold blast of air. Shivering, she rubbed her arms.

Ben got into the passenger seat, noticed her shivering, and immediately got out and took off his suit jacket, handing it to her. "Do you want me to go back in for your coat?"

She shook her head adamantly. "If you go back in, people will think they can come out and talk to me, and that's the last thing I want. I need to get away."

"Put my jacket on then, and you'll warm up a little."

She slipped her arms into the sleeves and was amazed at how dwarfed she felt. She was struck again at how huge Ben was compared to her. "Thank you." She loved to feel the warmth from his skin and smell him on the coat. "Okay, off to Rikki's place."

As she drove, she explained about the garage apartment. "Valerie and Jesse bought this place, and immediately started building the apartment for me. They wanted me to have a safe haven if I ever decided I couldn't stand being in Iowa, and they knew I was close. So, when Valerie talked me into moving here, which didn't take long, I had this beautiful, brand new apartment. I only stayed there for a few weeks, because I wasn't comfortable being there without Jesse and Valerie. I heard all these weird noises and freaked out regularly. So, Felicity invited me to move in with Linda, and I've been there ever since. I've gone back to Valerie's whenever she and Jesse were in town, but that was the only time."

"I'm excited to see it. You've said great things about it." He frowned for a moment. "You know that on a pastor's salary, we'll never really see the kind of wealth your sister has."

Rikki laughed. "I wouldn't know what to do with the kind of money she has."

"You really don't mind?"

"Not at all. If I want money, I can find a way to earn it. Maybe I'll go back to school."

"Really? Are you thinking about that?"

Rikki shrugged. "I never intended to drop out. I could finish my undergrad with online courses. I don't know though. I kind of like working at the bakery. Would it bother you if I went back to school? Or if I didn't?"

"I don't love you for your education or lack thereof. I love you for who you are. I don't care what you do for a living."

"What about kids?"

He looked over at her. "What about them?"

"Do you want them?"

"Not tomorrow, but sure, eventually they'd be nice."

She nodded. "Valerie said we need to have six, but I talked her down to three."

"Is it okay if I don't even ask?"

"Sure." She pulled into the driveway of the free-standing apartment on their land. The bottom floor was a two-car garage, and the upper was her place. As she pulled up, she realized her nerves were about to get the better of her, so she stayed sitting in the car for a moment after turning off the engine. "I haven't been here in a couple of weeks, so you'll have to forgive the dust and lack of food."

He shrugged. "Dusting is easy, and we'll eat breakfast at the bakery."

"I'll try to make time to stop after work to get some groceries."

"Just make a list, and I'll do it. It's easier for me, since I'll be in town anyway." He took her hand, lacing his fingers through hers. "I'm not going to judge you on your home-making skills or lack thereof."

She smiled at that, turning to him. "I can't believe I found a man who puts up with me like you do."

"Puts up with you? I beg to be with you!" He opened his door. "I'll carry your suitcases up."

"Thanks." She grabbed her shoulder bag from the back seat, carrying it up the stairs. Once she'd unlocked the door, she stepped inside, smiling when she saw all of her pretty things. The apartment was decorated perfectly in her eyes, and she was thrilled she now got to live there full time.

When she heard Ben's footsteps behind her, her heart started beating faster, almost painfully in her chest. Her breathing accelerated until she was taking short breaths and not getting enough air. She leaned against the wall, recognizing all the symptoms for exactly what they were. She was having a panic attack on her wedding night. Who did that?

She moved to the couch, leaning forward with her forearms against her thighs, trying to slow her breathing. Why had she thought she could go through with a wedding night? She knew better. She was a mess, and he should get their marriage annulled before it was too late.

She looked at him and shook her head, tears coursing down her cheeks. "I can't. I thought I could, but I just can't. I'm so sorry!"

10

Ben stared at her, trying to comprehend what was happening with Rikki. What couldn't she do? He walked over to sit beside her on the couch, and wrapped an arm around her shoulders. "Tell me what's wrong. What can't you do?"

She shook her head. "I can't go through with the wedding night. I thought I could, but—I'm so sorry. I just can't!"

Ben looked at her for a moment, closing his eyes as he dealt with her words. "That's all right."

"It is?" She looked at him as if he'd lost his mind.

"It is. I knew it was a possibility when I married you. I hoped you'd find that you weren't frightened, but I'm not even surprised."

"You're not?" She was, and she realized she shouldn't have been. New situations were hard for her, and even though this was Ben, she couldn't go through with it. Not yet. "Do you want to get an annulment?"

"Of course not! I married you because I love you. Yes, I eventually want sex. I want it tonight. I'm a red-blooded male after all. But I'm not going to insist when I know it will cause you anxiety. We'll wait."

"Are you real?"

He laughed. "Sure, I'm real. Don't think I don't hate this, because I do. I just understand. We'll spend some time getting to know each other, and then you'll be able to make love. I hope."

"I will. I know I will. Time is what I need."

"Then time is what you'll get." He kissed the top of her head, and sighed. "I'm going to sit right here while you get ready for bed. Wear something that's not revealing please."

"You're still planning to sleep with me?" she asked, surprised.

He nodded. "Unless you have a spare room you'd rather I was in."

"I have one, but there's no bed." She thought about it for a moment before nodding. "Okay. We're adults. I've been looking forward to sleeping in your arms for too long to tell you that you have to sleep on the couch."

He laughed. "I wouldn't agree to that anyway. This couch is way too short for me. I'd take the floor over the couch."

She got to her feet. "I'm going to go wash my face, brush my teeth, and get in bed. I'll let you know when I'm done in the bathroom, and you can come in." She rushed through her nightly routine, and when she left the bathroom to get into bed, she called out to him before sliding under the covers. She lay on her side as she heard him come into the bedroom and then close the bathroom door.

When he came out of the bathroom, he was wearing a pair of sweat pants and a T-shirt. "This is the best I can do. I don't own pajamas."

She looked over at him and smiled. "That's perfect." She was wearing a pair of pink pajamas with panda bears on them, and she felt a little silly, because who wore that on her wedding night, but he didn't complain.

He came to the bed and slid in beside her, his arm pulling her close to him. "If I do something that scares you, let me know. I just want to hold you."

Rikki sighed. "I know that's a lie."

"Okay, I want more than that, but that's all I'm going to do tonight. Even if you beg me on one knee to tear your clothes off and ravish your body, I'm going to just hold you."

She giggled. "Sounds good." She rested her head on his shoulder, and he stroked her back softly through her pajamas. It felt good to be so close to him. "What did you think of Brother Anthony's tirade during the wedding?"

He laughed. "It was very Brother Anthony. The man is crazy." He stroked her hair away from her face, loving that she was lying there and just letting him touch her. Trust had to come first, and eventually they'd make love. It didn't have to happen tonight though, as much as he wished it could. "Why don't you shut the light off?"

Rikki rolled away from him to turn off the lamp on her nightstand, before returning to rest with her head on his shoulder. "This is nice."

He smiled and kissed the top of her head. "I couldn't agree more. I'm going to enjoy sleeping with you as much as I'll enjoy making love with you."

"Are you sure about that?"

Ben laughed. "Okay, almost as much!"

Their first rehearsal was Friday night, because they'd had to cancel on Wednesday, and Lovie had insisted the two of them needed another night alone before they would be ready to direct the children.

After work on Friday, Rikki headed into town to help out with the pageant. She couldn't believe just how sweet and gentle Ben was with her, even though they'd yet to make love. He'd done the grocery shopping as promised and had praised her cooking. In bed, he held her close, but did no more than stroke her over her clothes. She felt guilty that she hadn't been able to make love with him, but she was getting more comfortable every day.

She worked with some of the children on their singing, while he worked with others on the play. Together, they'd be able to get the whole thing done. The nativity would be the easiest part, because the children didn't really need to act for it.

He followed her home from the rehearsal in good spirits. He could tell she was getting more and more comfortable with him. He truly hadn't been surprised when she'd refused to make love with him—disappointed yes, but not surprised.

He gave her a few minutes to get ready for bed as usual, and when she called to let him know it was his turn in the bathroom, he changed into the sweats and T-shirt he'd been sleeping in. When he came out, he saw that she was bundled under the covers completely.

He slid into bed and reached for her as he always did, but was surprised when he encountered more skin than usual. He wanted to tell her to go put on more clothes, but he couldn't do that to her. He could make it through the night with her half-clothed if she could.

He pulled her to him, his hands stroking over the silky thing she was wearing, wanting to reach down and see how much of her it covered, but he didn't dare. He didn't want to scare her.

"How'd the singing go?" he asked.

"Pretty well. I think our two soloists are going to kill it. I'm not sure about the others killing anything but the ears of the audience." She pressed a kiss to his shoulder. "What about the play?"

He shrugged. "The kids were good. They did what they were told and they did it well. There was a small fight between two of the boys because they both thought they should be standing closer to the audience, because their mothers had told them they should be seen. I took care of it."

"How?"

"I put them both behind another boy who wasn't fighting."

"Good solution!" She stared at him in the darkness, wondering why he wasn't making a move. She'd worn her sexy nightgown she'd bought for their wedding night. Couldn't he tell that was a sign that he should initiate lovemaking with her?

"I was pretty proud of it." He stroked his hand up her bare arm, wishing she wasn't so frightened. Lying in bed with her with so few clothes on wasn't going to be easy. "I like this thing you're wearing. Is it new?"

"It is. I got it for our wedding night."

"So, that's why it's so sexy. I wish you'd been able to wear it. I would have loved to see you in it."

"Oh really? So, you don't think you'd have wanted to take it off me?" She felt like she was having to lead him around by the nose to get him to understand she was ready. What was he waiting for?

"Is that an invitation?" Could she really be saying what he thought she was saying? Or was it just wishful thinking?

"I thought I was going to have to run out tomorrow and have one engraved to send you for you to figure it out." She shook her head at him, laughter in her voice.

"Are you sure?" he asked, propping himself on one elbow and looking at her. "You know you can stop me anytime."

"Just kiss me." She reached out and wrapped her arms around his neck, taking care of the kissing part herself. She pressed her mouth to his, her tongue stroking his top lip.

Ben didn't need to be told twice. His hands began stroking her insistently, one of them going under the hem of the flimsy little thing she was wearing. He still didn't know what it was called, but at the moment, he didn't care much either. He stroked her hip, while his other hand cupped her breast, his thumb finding her nipple and bringing it to a peak.

Rikki moved closer to him, one of her legs thrown over both of his. "I love you," she said softly, needing him to hear the words.

"I love you so much. Don't feel like you have to do this." He wanted her desperately, but he didn't want her to feel forced into making love with him. He continued stroking her, his hands belying his words.

"I don't feel forced into anything. You made it very clear that you'd still love me whether I was able to make love with you or not. That's all I really needed from you."

"Good."

There was no more talk for a long time after that, both of them too busy to think about words.

Afterward, they lay snuggled together on the bed, her head pillowed on his shoulder as it had been the past two nights, but tonight, she felt a contentment that surprised her. "I could do that again," she said with a grin.

He laughed. "I hope so, because I have a feeling once is not going to be enough for me."

She pressed a kiss to his bare shoulder, surprised at how comfortable she felt being completely naked with him. "Thank you for making me feel so loved. I don't think you have any idea what you've done for me, and thank you will never feel adequate to express my appreciation."

He sighed. "I don't want you to thank me. I just want you to be happy. You mean so much to me."

She sighed contentedly. "Who would have thought I'd find love with an associate pastor in Culpepper, Wyoming? I still can't get over it."

"Hey, pastors can make love too!"

She smiled closing her eyes. "They sure can."

"So happy you figured out you could do this. I worried that I'd be missing out forever."

EPILOGUE

Rikki sat in the front row of the church beside Ben, waiting for the children to file in for the pageant. It was Christmas Eve, the night they'd all been waiting for.

The music started, and Corinne led the others onto the stage, leaping and twirling as she went. Rikki had fought with her for a while over the butterfly wings, but she'd finally given in. After all, what was a Christmas pageant without butterfly wings on the ballerina?

Most of the children did well, but as Linda had said, there were a few that just couldn't seem to get with the program. Little Timmy Pfaffenbach decided to say the other wise men's lines, because he didn't have any of his own.

Little Georgie Bob Allen decided to do an impromptu song, and his voice wasn't bad, but he didn't sing a Christmas song. In fact, *Bubba Shot the Juke Box* didn't seem to be a song that should be sung in church at all in Rikki's opinion, but he got too many cheers for them to stop him.

And when Molly Dickens started cartwheeling across the stage, Rikki could only laugh helplessly.

After the performance, the parents all said what a delight it was that they'd strayed so far from the traditional program the church did every year, and all Ben could do was nod. He hadn't intended to stray from the program at all. It was as if the children had been rehearsing a different pageant than he'd been directing, but it was a hit. Maybe they'd have to do it all the same way next year.

After all, nothing seemed to go according to plan in their Culpepper Christmas, but it went the way it was obviously supposed to. Rikki had not only broken out of her shell, she had not had a panic attack since her wedding night, even though she was around people a lot more than she had been. Life was exciting enough without that.

She smiled up at Ben, thrilled to have him beside her. Life was good.

ABOUT THE AUTHOR

kirstenandmorganna.com

ALSO BY KIRSTEN OSBOURNE

Sign up for instant notification of all of Kirsten's New Releases
Text 'BOB' to 42828

And

For a complete list of Kirsten's works head to her website
wwww.kirstenandmorganna.com

Made in the USA
San Bernardino, CA
12 February 2018